Legend of the White Lion

Kathy Coons

outskirts
press

Outskirts Press, Inc.
http://www.outskirtspress.com

ISBN: 978-1-9772-1234-4

Cover Image by Shutterstock

Outskirts Press and the "OP" logo are trademarks belonging to Outskirts Press, Inc.

PRINTED IN THE UNITED STATES OF AMERICA

This book is dedicated to my daughters, sister Judy, and my husband, from the bottom of my heart.

CHAPTER ONE

It was very long ago, and early spring made the northern territory lush and green. The bushes and undergrowth dripped wet with the morning rain.

The mornings had become much warmer. Daylight now came peeking slowly over the white-topped mountains. The bright sun made the raindrops on the leaves and bushes sparkle and glisten.

The tall Native American man Kawada walked the thin trail many times hunting for food for his family. He could feel the cool air on his face. Kawada enjoyed the beauty of the forest and had his mind on the hunt. Today he would try to get a deer so his wife could cook and serve the village to celebrate the birth of their new son.

It was Kawada's dream to have a son who could hunt and fish with him. He grinned and thought to himself how handsome his new son was when he first saw him. Kawada was deep in thought and not aware of the large creature waiting for the best moment to attack.

The white lion waited until the Native American man came closer to him. It dug its powerful claws in the moist grass and leaped with its mouth open, aiming for the man's neck. If the lion could accomplish reaching the man's neck, its jaws and teeth would crush bone and sever veins and arteries, killing its prey instantly.

The young Native American woman Nooka awoke from her dream and sat straight up. The dream had seemed so real. Her hair was wet with perspiration as she tried to recall the dream. She was shaken and couldn't control her trembling. Nooka woke before the lion's jaws had reached her brother Kawada. What did this dream mean? Her dreams always meant something. Sometimes events would be exact or sometimes a mysteriously similar event would occur. She would always tell the tribe's shaman and together they warned the tribe of bad things to come.

The large white mountain lion had come down from the mountain looking for food. The winter in the mountain had been harsh and hunger overran the fear of man. The lion had killed only to feed itself and was driven by a force of nature that couldn't be explained.

The young Native American woman had started dreaming of it long before it came. She had dreamed of it snatching away children and old women who went off on their own to look for berries and roots. This lately had come true. A woman in the tribe had seen the white lion kill her sister while they were picking berries. This confirmed the legend told around the tribal fires of a white lion sent by the mountain to terrorize the valley.

Children were not to go out of the camp now and men hunted in groups. When women went to get water by the river or to gather berries and roots, they never went alone. A man from the tribe would always go with them, ready for the white lion to attack.

Nooka ran to the shaman's lodge. Rushing in, she quickly told the shaman of her dream.

He always listened to the dreams of the young Native American woman and had concluded Mother Earth sometimes did things to remind man just how vulnerable he was. It had been a long time since a white lion had come to the valley. He remembered old tribesmen telling about years ago when a similar white lion had come to the valley, picking off the tribesman one by one. The legend was told that only the firstborn, of a firstborn could stop the reign of terror. And the chosen one would always be a woman. There were several in the village and the shaman wasn't sure who would be the chosen one. Nooka had told him she dreamed it was her.

The tribe had sent many search parties out hoping to hunt down the large cat but came back telling the rest of the tribe they could see no trace of the cat and it had disappeared and couldn't be found. Many had tried to track the cat only to have the tracks go for a while and then just disappear. They had named the white lion Nakano, the ghost cat.

The shaman hoped soon the mountain god would guide the chosen one on how to rid the mountain of the white lion. The tribe could not afford to lose any more. Many tribesman, women, and children had been lost from the last harsh winter. Their tribe was now very small, and many women and children were left without a man to hunt or keep them.

The old shaman sat and listened to the young Native American woman's dream, trying to interpret what it meant. He looked straight ahead and said, "Nooka, this dream, we must warn your brother of the danger. We must go find him."

They left the lodge and went directly to her brother's lodge. Kawada's wife called back when they called out for Kawada. She was feeding her new son and encouraged them to enter. "Kawada has gone out hunting this morning. He should be back soon."

Nooka's heart sank. She knew she would never see her brother again. Sadly, she left the lodge and went to ready herself to go find her brother. She must find out for sure. Hurriedly she armed herself with a bow and arrow and strapped a knife to her leg.

The old shaman warned her to stay and let the men try to find him. She patted the old man's shoulder and said, "I have dreamed of chasing this Nakano many times. I know it is I who will have to find and kill it." She turned and left the old man.

The old shaman wiped the tear that slipped down his face. He was sure he would never see Nooka again.

The young Native American woman searched the valley most of the morning until she found her brother's footprint in the moist forest floor. She was sure it was his footprint, he had to be close.

Why would he venture out without another tribesman? But she knew of her brother's stubbornness. How could she judge him? Here she was by herself out in the forest. She remembered the dream she had many times of her running after the large white cat and knew this was her destiny.

She heard something move in front of her. She stopped to listen. The forest was dense, and she could see nothing. She realized the only way she would be able to see was to climb a tree. Climbing high, she rested on a large branch. Above the trees a storm was brewing quickly. The clouds above her swirled and the wind started blowing. The rain hit her hard in the face.

Nooka scanned the forest until she saw the large cat dragging his kill. She could easily identify what it was—it was a half-eaten human corpse. Her breathing stopped. She watched the cat try to hide it under the bushes. Bile rose in her throat, but she swallowed it down.

The rain increased to a downpour and the wind blew hard, waving the branches of the tree. Nooka hung on for dear life. She watched as the lion came in her direction. Did he see her and know she was there? The lion was close now, but all Nooka could do was hold on tight so she wouldn't get blown out of the tree. He looked up at her and their eyes locked.

A large gust of wind blew and snapped the branch Nooka was on. It came crashing down and fell over the large cat, knocking it unconscious. Nooka gathered herself up and pulled out the knife she had strapped on her leg and sunk it deep into the exposed stomach of the cat, killing it. Nooka sat there watching the red blood come out of the cat and the rain wash it away from the snow-white fur.

She was not sure how long she sat there but a voice brought her back to reality. "Nooka, are you all right?" A tall Native American man named Wandok stood above her. "Nooka, are you OK?"

"Yes," she managed to say. Wandok took the knife from her hand and helped her stand. "Kawada's body is just over there." She said as she looked at the warrior. She noticed the look of disbelief on his face as he stared at the white cat she had slain.

"You must skin the cat and take back the pelt. The tribe needs to know the cat is dead. I will show you how," Wandok explained. He was amazed at how this small woman could hunt down and kill the cat that had eluded all the men in the tribe. He took a deep breath and explained, "Take the knife and cut here." He patiently instructed and helped Nooka skin the massive cat. "We will come back and get your brother's body and have a burial ceremony. I am sad Kawada doesn't walk with us anymore."

Wandok told her, "You must carry the pelt into the village. You were the one who stopped the cat from killing any more of our tribe. This is the legend told by those who lived before us."

Nooka lifted the heavy pelt and walked into the village. The tribe surrounded her in celebration. For now, the legend of the white lion was at rest until Mother Earth saw the need to send it back to the valley again.

Washington State, Early 1970s

The winter had been hard, so the large cat was forced to come down the mountain to look for larger game. Hunger drove the animal lower and lower down. Nearly a week had passed since the last big kill and the past few days it had survived only on small rodents. It easily jumped to a rocky ledge to sniff for food. A strange new smell drifted through the air and all the large animal's senses were immediately alerted. Suddenly the source of the scent came into view directly under the ledge. With no hesitation, it dropped on the moving target, killing it almost instantly. Caution gave way to hunger and even though it was still daylight in an open area it began to eat. By the time darkness fell over the valley the immense animal had eaten its fill and lay beside the prey, protecting it from other predators.

Without warning the sensitive ears picked up an unfamiliar sound approaching the area. The strange sound was confusing and before it could react, a large logging truck roared around the corner of the dirt road and the two men in the truck were awestruck at the scene in front of their headlights. They had watched the lion streak off into the thick undergrowth.

"My God," yelled the driver, Jim, as he stomped the brake, trying not to hit the half-eaten corpse on the side of the road. "Was that a white mountain lion?" he asked his passenger, Ed.

Ed exclaimed, "I saw it! In a blink it was gone! Where is your gun, Jim? God damn, it's a man-killer!"

Jim jumped out of the truck and grabbed his gun from behind the seat. Gingerly he stepped over to see if he could recognize the half-eaten body. "Damn Ed, its Jeb Hart. Damn cat must have got him when he was trying to walk home from fishing. Let's load him up in the back of the truck and take him on into town. If we leave him here the cat will come back and—" He swallowed hard and cleared his throat. He was unable to finish his sentence when the scream of the cat came piercing though the night.

The scream of the cat echoed through the rocky and wooded area of the valley floor. Ed could feel the hair on the back of his neck stick up. "He was white, wasn't he Jim?" he asked as they unfolded the tarp to wrap the body in.

"Yeah, yeah, he was white—big son of a bitch too. Had to

be one of the biggest cats I have ever seen," Jim said as he attempted to keep his emotions under control and his stomach from losing its contents as they rose in his throat again.

They quickly finished the gruesome task of lifting the body onto the tarp and loading it into the truck.

"Remember the legend of the Nakano?" Jim asked as he recalled the storytelling of the old Native American woman in town.

"Suppose it's true?" asked Ed. "How rare do you think a white cat is?"

They both recalled the legend as they drove to town. As they both talked about the legend, the logging truck roared closer to town.

"Maybe we are getting a little carried away," mused Jim. "That old Native American woman is crazy and old as dirt. Let's take the body to old Doc's." He quickly said, changing the subject.

Both were silent for the rest of ride to town.

The truck arrived at Doc's house in a cloud of dust. Doc ran out of the house and yelled, "What the heck are you boys doing? Have you been drinking and driving that big old truck?" Doc stood on his porch shaking his fist at them. His few hairs on his head stood straight up and his potbelly strained against his shirt buttons.

Doc's wife Betty had died two summers ago, which meant he could eat his favorite food any time he wanted to. You could see him every morning buying his morning cinnamon rolls. The small logging town and the surrounding countryside was very lucky to have any kind of a doctor, and everyone loved old Doc.

The nearest hospital was hundreds of miles away so people from miles around would come to visit him for medical help. He really needed a nurse badly, but old Gertie did the books and sometimes, although she hated to, would help him with patients. Anything too serious he would send to Seattle.

Ed jumped out of the truck and pulled back the tarp. He told Doc the story of how they found old Jeb's body and the white lion they had seen. By the end of the story old Ed was crying. "Doc, you have got to get a hold of the Harts and let them know about old Jeb."

"Yes, yes I will. You boys go on home. Please don't let this out and be telling anyone until the sheriff talks to you." Doc stressed. Doc immediately called the sheriff when the two men left.

When the sheriff arrived at Doc's, he listened to the story Ed and Jim had told about the white lion. The sheriff would go talk to Ed and Jim, and he was sure he would find both men at McCain's Tavern. The sheriff knew this needed to be kept secret until he knew all the facts. The sheriff's six-foot-four frame carried his large muscular body very well but even he was teary-eyed looking over old Jeb's body. He rubbed his face and combed back his black hair, putting his hat back on.

"That's the worst thing I have ever seen in all my years of practicing medicine," said Doc, visibly shaken. Jeb had been a family friend of his for years. "Sheriff, you can take him to the morgue. I'll call the family and go out there tomorrow. They should hear it from me."

"OK, Doc," the sheriff said.

The sheriff dropped the body off at the morgue and told George, who owned the funeral home, to please keep this quiet. He drove off to find Ed and Jim. He was sure they were already on their second or third beer and he hoped they had not told the whole place.

The sheriff entered the tavern and soon spotted both of men setting in the back. There were two empty beer glasses in front of each of them and both had started in on the third. So much for making sure they hadn't been drinking, the sheriff thought to himself.

"Over here, Sheriff," yelled out Ed.

"Boys, have you told anyone?" he asked, looking hard at them.

Ed spoke up first. "No, no. We just came in and ordered. Sheriff, it was awful, just awful." As he went on the story poured out of him.

The sheriff listened without questions and quietly said, "Tomorrow I want you to show me exactly where you found Jeb—and bring your rifles."

The sheriff left, mulling over the story the two men had told him. He recalled the legend of the Nakano and took a deep breath, not knowing what to believe. He looked out of his patrol truck window at the beautiful crisp night. The hard Washington winter had pulled the white lion down from the mountains and it now had a taste of human blood. It would be hard to encourage it into leaving and it would have to be killed. He was glad Doc would tell Jeb Hart's family, but it will probably be just as difficult to find good help to hunt down the man-eater. This could become a very dangerous situation. Almost everyone in the valley had a gun.

The small logging valley would come together, he was sure, but he didn't want it to get out of hand and someone get hurt.

The thought of the old Native American woman's tale again flooded his thoughts. He remembered his dad telling the tale. He took another deep breath and forced the thought from his mind.

This small community would need a lot of support from the local sheriff. He stopped in his driveway and let the truck continue to run. It would be a hard thing to go to Jeb's funeral. A great guy, Jeb had never married. He and his brother Henry owned the logging company here in the valley and his death would surely need some closure. The Harts were a fine, upstanding family in the valley and old Jeb would have done anything for anyone. The sheriff drew in another long hard breath. He would go out to Henry's first thing tomorrow with Doc.

The large cat found shelter on a high rock ledge where it lay cleaning itself after its feast. It had returned to the site to move the kill but after several minutes of searching the area it returned to the high rocks for a nap. With a full stomach the cat slept easily and would not need another meal for couple of days.

CHAPTER TWO

I n a small town in Kansas a young woman sat at her mother's funeral. She thought about the last few days. She had sold all the furniture in the house to pay for medicine for her mother. All was sold but her bed.

When the funeral was finally over, Mariah watched them lower her mother's casket into the grave. Two years she had cared for her dying mother. Mariah worked part time in the county hospital until the last month when her mother turned worse needing twenty-four-hour care. Sadness hit her heart. Now she had no more family, no one. Mariah felt very alone after the funeral as she drove her mother's old car to the lawyer's office. She wondered if her father was still alive. She knew very little about him. Her mother had told her he was from somewhere around Omaha and had left her before Mariah was born. Her mother moved back to Kansas to live with her parents. Mariah had watched both her grandparents pass and now her mother was gone. Tears filled her eyes, but she held them back swallowing hard.

As she parked the car in front of the lawyer's office, she could not imagine anything would be left in her mother's estate after her long illness. Mariah had quit nursing school and a good job to move back home to take care of her mother. The diagnosis was lung cancer. It had been two long years out of her life, but she loved her mother and hoped she had been somewhat of a comfort to her during her last days.

She sat in the parked car a few minutes and went through the two years she had cared for her mother. Mariah shook her head and came back to reality; she needed to finish up her mother's affairs. Looking across the flat fields, she wondered, now what?

Mariah had seen an ad in the paper about a position in Seattle, Washington. A young doctor and his wife needed a nanny for their two children. She had called yesterday and decided to see them next week. Mariah would take her time and drive up there. The young couple would give her room and board and a small wage. The wage was more than she ever dreamed she could get anywhere else. When she had enough money, she would go back to nursing school.

As she shut the car door and walked up to the lawyer's door, she hoped her mother had thought about saving a little back to help her get back on her feet. Walking inside the door of the hot and stuffy office, the smell of wet dog hit her nostrils. She walked over to her mother's lawyer Walter Seth and offered him her hand. His large and very fat bulldog sat on a chair in the corner.

"Thanks for coming, Mariah; this will not take long," Walter said holding onto her hand a little too long after the handshake. He thought she was one of the most beautiful women in town. He thought her long, dark brown hair and large, dark brown eyes, and light complexion made her stunning. She didn't look anything like her mother, who was blond and blue eyed. He noticed Mariah's outfit. It must have been her mother's. It fit her well around her tall, slim frame. "Sit and we will get through this. Your mother had very little. Her bank account is gone after paying for the funeral expenses. She had me do a reverse mortgage on her home, which is like selling your home but still living in it. This is the money she used for doctor bills and other expenses. Basically, all there is left is her old car and a few hundred dollars." Walter watched Mariah for a reaction. She was stunned but decided with transportation and a little money she would be OK.

"What are you going to do with yourself?" Walter asked.

"I saw an ad in the paper for nannies up in Seattle, Washington." Mariah said. "I called and got the job. I am to be there next week. I am going to be a nanny and go to school part-time."

"How are you going to get there?" Walter asked.

"I will be driving Mom's car," stated Mariah.

Seth chuckled, "I'm not so sure that old car has that many miles left in it. It probably should be junked. I wouldn't advise it."

"I will be fine," retorted Mariah already thinking of the trip.

"Well, sounds like you are as strong willed as your mother. Here is what is left of the money." He handed her two hundred dollars and said, "I want to wish you the very best. It is a fine thing you did taking care of your mom these past couple years."

With that, Mariah was off to her mother's house to pack the car with clothes, some food, and a few things her mother left her. She was kind of excited. This would be an adventure, something she had not experienced in a long time. Mariah knew Kansas was not where she would live out her life. She had dreamed she was floating over mountains and tall trees since early childhood, seeing lush and beautiful countryside. In the dream, many times she was awakened by yellow eyes that would pop up in the dream; she would wake up in a cold sweat. She had never told anyone of these dreams. But she knew this small little Kansas town was not her destiny. Paying the last of her and her mother's bills she counted the rest of the money and was ready to leave her childhood home.

The sun was just coming over the horizon as Mariah left Kelly's gas station with a full tank of gas and high hopes, turning to take a final look at the small town where she grown up. It was a dying town. All the young people were moving to the city. There were a lot of nice people here, but there were no opportunities.

"Goodbye," she said aloud as she took off down the road, feeling a little apprehensive for the first time. This was the first time she had been out of the state of Kansas. She could feel the invisible pull of something, and she followed it, not looking back again.

Mariah drove all day. She ended up at a rest stop in Utah where she slept in the car overnight. The car had used a lot of gas but still seemed to be running fine. She dreamed again of floating over mountains. It was night and the moon shone just enough to see the treetops on the mountain side. She floated just like she did most nights, up and down the mountains. Suddenly a pair of yellow eyes jumped out at her again. She awoke breathing heavily and very shaken. Mariah soon remembered where she was and looked out at the beauty of the morning. Sitting outside on the hood of the car she ate the last of her food. Again, she felt an invisible pull. When she was finished eating, she drove off and soon left the state of Utah. There were many more miles ahead of her, but a serene feeling came over her like she hadn't had for a long time.

The end of the second day brought her to a small town in Washington called Elk Lake. Just as she was leaving the city limits the car started making terrible sounds. After checking the map, she determined there was not another town for over one hundred miles and it was getting dark, so she turned around and drove back to Elk Lake. She immediately spotted a sign that said, "Cub's Garage" and pulled the now-smoking car up to the door. The garage was closed for the night, so she had no choice but to spend the night in the driveway. She counted the remaining money and was distressed to find she had only $51.35 left to her name. Seattle was still a long way and she could not even guess how much it would take to fix the car. Never one to dwell on problems before they happened, Mariah stepped out of the car and went for a walk to check out the town. She smiled to herself after going five blocks down the main street—this town was smaller than the one she had just left two days ago. There was only an occasional car driving on main street and very few lights on in the houses. It was around ten o'clock and apparently bedtime. The only activity seemed to be music and laughter coming from a bar named McCain's Tap. On the outskirts of town, she came to a beautiful, glassy lake with the Milky Way reflecting off the shining water. She heard an eerie scream echoing across the water. It frightened her for a moment, but she decided it must be a bird of some kind. As she turned to leave, she noticed the town sign: Elk Lake, population 651.

She was starting to shiver in the cold night air, so she hurried back to the car and pulled the blankets up around her neck. Her stomach growled with hunger, but sleep would take precedence over hunger this night. Just as she was about to surrender to sleep, she heard some men talking as they left McCain's Tap.

"Too bad about Jeb," she heard one of them say, "He must have decided to do some fishing and met up with the big cat. It ripped him from stem to stern according to Doc—nothing left of his innards!" Mariah shuddered as the man continued, "Sounds like Jeb finally met his match. The Hart family is offering a two-thousand-dollar reward to bag that big white lion."

"We ought to go out there and try to collect that reward, don't you think? Two thousand dollars is a lot of money. Ever shot a lion before?" she heard one of the men slur.

Now barely audible, the other man answered, "No, but there is always a first time."

"A white lion?" Mariah said out loud as she covered her head with the blanket. "What kind of a place is this the jungle?" Finally, her shaking subsided and sleep came.

In the wooded area high on a rocky ledge the cat licked his snow-white fur, trying to erase all blood stains from his recent kill. He had earlier killed a sheep in a nearby pasture. The white lion yawned and stretched, the extensive muscles rippling down its back. He fell into a deep sleep. Food was plentiful here and would keep him from traveling very far.

CHAPTER THREE

Mariah was awakened by a tap on the window. She opened her eyes to see a Native American man with a ponytail staring at her. She jumped up, trying to regain her senses and remembered where she was. As she unlocked the door and jumped out of the car she meekly asked, "Are you the owner of the garage?"

"Yes, my name is Cub," he said with no change of expression. His dark brown eyes bore through her until she had to turn her head. He was very handsome. She could not help but see through his tight T-shirt his large muscular chest and arms.

"I'm headed for Seattle. My car needs a little work. Could you look at it?" she asked with a smile. The Native American man said nothing and showed no expression as he went around the car to look under the hood.

"I don't have much money, but I don't think it is serious," Mariah said, although she was getting a little nervous thinking of what she would do if she was unable to drive the car. But her thought was interrupted by the sheriff's truck driving up and coming to a sliding stop.

The sheriff stood up out of the truck and tipped his hat to Mariah and spoke to Cub, "I want to ask you if you would try to track the white cat, the one that killed old Jeb two nights ago? The Hart family is willing to pay two thousand dollars to the one who bags it."

Cub looked through the sheriff, again never changing his expression. Mariah saw Cub's jaw muscles tighten under the dark skin. He had high cheekbones and dark, piercing eyes. He was not nearly as tall as the sheriff but much more muscular.

"Sheriff, you know my people's belief. It is a spirit. It has been passed down for many generations. There is nothing you can do but wait." Cub calmly stated and again turned his attention back to Mariah's car.

"Damn it, Cub, you're the best tracker around. I saw the prints. No spirit makes footprints, do they?" asked the sheriff.

"If they have taken on a body," Cub said, quietly lifting his head up from working on Mariah's car to look straight at the sheriff, "Yes, then they will have prints."

"Good Lord, Cub! If you're not going to help me, fine. Just don't go into the forest alone," The sheriff said as he stomped off tipping his hat once again to Mariah.

Cub stood up from looking under Mariah's hood and said, "Your car is no good." Looking straight at her and continued, "It is done; the engine is gone."

Mariah blinked, and knowing very little about cars, Mariah told him to put a different engine in the car. For the first time Cub smiled from ear to ear, showing his dazzling white teeth. "No, I don't have one. You don't have enough money anyway. I will tow the car out back to my junk lot and maybe someone will buy parts."

Feeling dejected Mariah unloaded all her earthly belongings from the car, which fit in a small bag. She let out a long sigh and asked Cub how much she owed him.

"Nothing," he said, "But if you are headed to Seattle it will cost for a bus ticket. Course you would also have to find a ride to a town that has a bus and the closest is Everett, nearly 120 miles in the other direction."

Mariah sat her things down on the driveway and let out a big sigh. "That is just great. Are there any rooms around here?"

"No, no rooms. You might want to look on the bulletin board in the laundromat." Cub said, feeling a little sorry for her at this point.

Mariah went over to the small laundromat and found a want ad reading, "Wanted: Woman to do housekeeping and care for small child." It was signed Cass Hart, and gave the phone number but no address. Mariah attempted to call on the pay telephone but didn't get an answer. She again walked back to Cub's Garage. She found Cub still bent over, looking under the hood of her mother's car, "Do you know Cass Hart and how I could get a hold of him? I found an ad pinned up about him needing someone to watch a child. That is what I am going to Seattle to do, besides taking a few classes. I have experience! I tried to call the number, but no one answered. Do you know how to get a hold of him?" Mariah asked again, letting out a big sigh.

"Yes, I know him. I should warn you that he is not a pleasant fellow. The great spirits took his wife after she gave birth to a little girl about five years ago. Cass has five brothers, and all their children are boys. Cass's child is the only girl. It makes her kind of special to the family and Cass's reason for living. Other women attempted to care for the child, but Cass ran them off with his quick temper. If that hasn't scared you off, I will draw you a map to get to his house," Cub said, watching her.

"Do you think he will hire me?" Mariah asked.

Again, the handsome face smiled, "He will hire you. There are not too many women around these parts, and he has little choice left!" Cub drew the map and explained the directions. He offered his hand to shake and asked her, "What is your name?"

"Mariah, Mariah Brooke," she answered. This was the only time Mariah had seen a change in his expression aside from a few smiles. His face lit up as he looked down at her.

"The wind," he whispered. "The legend is revealing itself." With that he turned and walked away.

Mariah noticed how erect and proud he stood and could not help noticing his exquisite build again. She threw her pack full of everything she owned over her shoulder and started off in the direction of Cass Hart's home following Cub's map.

The cat awoke from a long nap around midmorning. It sat on its haunches and looked across the valley, sniffing the air. The large cat yawned and stretched and laid back down. After dozing off and on for a while in the warm sun it soon fell back into a deep sleep.

CHAPTER FOUR

Mariah looked for the first road that turned right after the bridge. According to Cub's map, that was the road where Cass Hart lived. It was now after noon and she was starving. The candy bar she had purchased in the laundromat was long gone and now she was thirsty, too. She could see the lake from the road and wondered if she dared drink from it. She was desperate so she stepped off the road and cut through the woods until she reached the shoreline of the lake. The water was cool as she drank, fed by the melting mountain snow. She was surprised as to how clear the water was and how she could see the bottom of the lake for a distance. As she turned back toward the road, she noticed large footprints in the mud. She didn't know a lot about animals, but there was no mistaking that this was the footprint of the cat the sheriff was talking about. She held her hand out and was in awe. The radius of the print was much larger than her hand.

Mariah gasped and drew her hand back. She shuddered as she remembered the sheriff telling Cub not to go into the forest alone. She was confused as to why Cub would encourage her to take off by herself. She again looked at the size of the print and felt the largeness of this creature. It was visible to her how the weight of the animal had caused it to sink into the mud. She tracked the animal and determined it had stopped here to drink. The edges of the track were not dry, which confirmed to her that the track was not very old. She immediately jumped up and ran back to the road. Soon it would be nightfall and she needed to hurry and find the house before this animal found her.

She checked the map again and wondered how far it was. She felt as if she had walked at least five miles. The area seemed so remote. There had been no houses or cars since the edge of town. As she crested a small hill the lake narrowed. Then she saw the bridge crossing that took the road over the lake. Just after she crossed the bridge, she looked for the small dirt road Cub had told her Cass Hart's house was on. Soon she found the road and was relieved knowing that she was almost there. Darkness was quickly approaching. She began to run.

There it is, she thought as she first viewed the roof of the large two-story home. The closer she got she could see the large porch that spread across the front of the house. Climbing the steps up on the porch, she could see a logging truck parked along the side of the house. A long bench sat on both sides of the front door. Soon Mariah grew weary of knocking on the door and sat down on one of the benches. Sighing and using her pack as a pillow she decided to rest for a moment. She would just wait for him. Her stomach growled and her feet throbbed, but she was asleep almost instantly.

The small child fell asleep on old Doc's lap on the way home from Henry Hart's house. She was such a beautiful child, Doc thought. Blond, blue-eyed, and petite, she was sure to be a heartbreaker. Doc remembered the day she was born. Becky, Cass's wife, had been a frail, sickly little thing. The child was the spitting image of her but healthy and rarely sick.

Becky should never have attempted pregnancy, but they had wanted a child so badly. Doc kept her bedridden for the last six weeks of the pregnancy, but the baby still came early. After several hours of grueling labor Becky's delicate body just gave up, only minutes after the birth. Her death about killed Cass but he was determined to raise Jenny on his own. She had been staying with his folks most of the time until last year. Cass now wanted her to live with him and he tried to care for her but looking at Jenny's matted hair Doc knew he needed some help but was too proud to ask. Doc had talked him into writing up an ad and placing it in the paper. Cass frowned on this because he wasn't sure about a stranger taking care of Jenny, after numerous local women just up and left. Doc tried to tell him it was because he was mean and never had a nice word to say about anyone. Nothing these women did was good enough; Cass had told him. Doc looked at the man that drove the truck. Cass was a mountain of a man and a good man. The death of Becky had changed him. Doc sighed and couldn't help the hurt in his heart for his longtime friend. He had tried a couple of times to play matchmaker with local women, but it always failed. Cass just wasn't ready yet. The pickings around here were getting fewer and fewer, but Doc was always keeping his eyes open! The child squirmed in her sleep and broke Doc's thoughts.

"You sure you want me to take your truck home, Cass?" Doc asked.

"Yeah, Jenny needs to go to bed. You can pick us up before Uncle Jeb's funeral in the morning, around seven thirty, OK?" replied Cass. He was thinking about finding something for Jenny to wear that was clean. He had turned down his sisters-in-law when they asked him if he needed help. He liked all four of them, but he hated it when they attempted to do too much for him. They all had families of their own and he felt they had enough to do. Jenny had lots of clothes he had purchased taking lumber into Everett. The problem was he just couldn't find the time to keep them clean and pressed. He had all he could do just trying to get her hair washed. The long, thin blond hair reminded him so much of her mother he refused to get it cut.

They drove up behind the logging truck parked beside Cass's house. Doc picked up Jenny and told Cass, "I'll carry her, and you get the dog."

Mariah awoke to a low growl. She opened her eyes to see

what looked like a wolf. Standing behind it was a giant of a man. She screamed and jumped up, then fainted.

"What the hell was that?" asked Doc running out of the house after putting Jenny to bed.

"It's a woman. I don't know who she is or what she's doing here," said a shocked Cass. "Better help me get her into the house." Cass picked Mariah up and carried her to the couch.

"Better move that stuff so I can lay her down, Doc."

"Boy, do you ever need someone to help keep this place cleaned up," scolded Doc as he moved things off the couch to make room for Mariah. "I don't know her either; wonder where she came from. I better check her over and see why she fainted."

Mariah opened her eyes just as Doc was unbuttoning her blouse.

"Hey, who are you?" she asked and grabbed the front of her blouse.

"I am a doctor, young lady. The question is who are you and what are you doing camped out on Cass's front porch?"

"I came here looking for a job. The man named Cub told me Mr. Hart was looking for a nanny for his little girl."

"So, you just waltzed out here and thought if you camped out on my porch you would get the job?" Mariah heard a gruff voice on the other side of the couch. She turned to see the large bearded man standing with his hands on his hips.

"Wait a minute, Cass. I think that is a good idea. You need some help with Jenny in the morning and your house is in shambles. No one from around here will help you because you are so mean and ornery. Hire the girl for a nanny and a house-keeper. If it doesn't work out in a couple of weeks, then let her go," Doc said to Cass. "You might not need the help, but Jenny does. Think of her."

Cass thought about it for a long time. Mariah was close to panic because now reality had hit, and it occurred to her that she might not have a job or a roof over her head tonight.

"We don't know anything about this woman. How do I know I can trust her in my house, and more important, with my daughter?" Cass argued.

"Can you tell us something about yourself, where you came from and how you ended up here?" questioned Doc.

Mariah recounted the last two years of her life briefly and when she finished, she felt like she had gained some trust from the two men. Doc liked her from the beginning and was very sympathetic about the illness and death of her mother and when she said she dropped out of nursing school a light bulb went off in his head.

"I'll give room and board in exchange for you cooking meals, taking care of my house, and my daughter. You can start first thing in the morning by getting her ready to go to a funeral. After two weeks we'll see if it is working," said Cass

"Now you're talking, Cass. What about it, young lady?" asked Doc, acting as the mediator. "Do you want to try it for a couple of weeks?"

"I don't have enough money to get to Seattle. If you decide you don't need me in two weeks will you make sure I get to Seattle?"

"You can always get Gus to take her in the logging truck at the end of the month," suggested Doc.

"Done, two weeks then. You can sleep here on the couch tonight," grumbled the bearded man.

Mariah could not help but notice that he didn't look at her but directed his conversation to Doc.

"Don't mind Cass; he was born cranky," Doc joked. "What did you say your name was again?"

"Mariah Brooke," she answered.

"Well Mariah, when was the last time you ate?" asked Doc.

"This morning I had a candy bar. That's probably why I fainted," offered Mariah, realizing she did feel a little weak.

"You got anything for her to eat, Cass?

"Jenny has some boxes of cold cereal or there are some

canned goods in the pantry. Everything else is frozen." With that Cass motioned for his dog to follow him as he headed for his bedroom, "Come, Wolf, time for bed. See you in the morning, Doc. Don't let the white cat get you!"

Doc sat at the table with Mariah as she ate two bowls of cereal.

"Is that a real wolf?" she asked.

"No, it is only part wolf but totally devoted to Cass and Jenny. Long as you don't appear to be a threat to them, he won't hurt you. Don't let Cass scare you. Once he gets to know you, he'll soften up. I'd better get going, and you need your rest. Jenny is an early riser," Doc said as he headed for the door.

Mariah heard the truck start up and was thinking of Cass's remark to Doc about the white cat but quickly fell asleep.

CHAPTER FIVE

Mariah awoke with the feeling someone was staring at her. She opened her eyes to see a tiny blond angel standing next to a wolf dog.

"Hi, what is your name?" asked the little girl.

"I'm Mariah. What is your name?" Mariah asked as she wiped the sleep from her eyes.

"My name is Jenny. I live here with my daddy. Does he know you are here?" she asked.

"Yes, I'm going to stay with you for a while and help take care of you. Is that OK?" asked Mariah, smiling at the angelic face.

"Would you help me find something to wear to my Uncle Jeb's funeral?"

"Sure thing," Mariah said as she reached down and took her tiny little hand. She followed Jenny to her room and Mariah had to blink in disbelief as she looked around the room. There were no sheets on the bed. Clothes and toys were scattered everywhere or piled high in a corner. The carpet and curtains were pink and needing a cleaning.

"This one looks OK, don't you think?" Jenny said, holding up a much-wrinkled dress she had pulled from a pile on the floor.

"Well, let me see," Mariah said looking the pink velvet dress over closely. "Do you have an ironing board?"

"Yeah, I'll show you," Jenny said, grinning.

Mariah grabbed another dress and removed a ruffled ribbon from its waist.

"Hey, what are you doing to that dress?" Jenny asked with a crinkle in her forehead.

"I'm going to make you a ribbon for your hair," explained Mariah. "First let's get the wrinkles out of these."

Jenny led Mariah through the kitchen to the laundry room. The kitchen was a disaster. Dirty dishes and pans were stacked everywhere. She saw the small area that Doc had cleaned off on the table last night so she could eat her cereal. This would be one of the first things I will take care of, Mariah thought to herself.

"The iron is somewhere under these clothes," said Jenny.

"Are those clean or dirty clothes?" asked Mariah.

"I don't know," said Jenny. "Just throw them over there in a pile.

Mariah had to giggle at her as she helped Jenny clean the clothes off the ironing board. She quickly pressed Jenny's dress and ribbon.

"Do you have any socks and shoes that will go with this dress?"

Jenny smiled and ran out of the room. She returned quickly with a pair of black patent leather shoes and white socks with pink trim.

"These are perfect." Mariah said to Jenny, amazed she could find them so quickly in the unorganized room she had just been in.

"Mariah, do you think you could make my daddy's shirt look good, too? It's all crinkled like my dress," Jenny said as she pointed to the shirt hanging next to a black suit.

Mariah started ironing the shirt and showed Jenny how to polish her Daddy's shoes. Jenny was excited to help. She jabbered the whole time to Mariah.

"I only have five uncles now. Old Jeb was my great uncle, Gumpa's brother. Daddy has five brothers: Gus, Will, Matt, Mike, and little Jeb. Matt and Mike are twins. They're all married except little Jeb; he is too young. My mommy went to heaven so I could live. My Grammy isn't feeling well. Daddy says she is too stubborn to go to heaven for a while. I have lots of cousins. They are all boys," Jenny said, going on and on.

"OK, all done. Now let's get you cleaned up," said Mariah

As Mariah walked by the porch window, she noticed the sun was just coming up. What a gorgeous view, she thought. The light fog hung over the water, and the light was just spreading across the lake that was as smooth as glass. The trees mirrored into the water from the other side as a perfect reflection. There were mountains behind the lake and dense forest everywhere. To the right of the glassed-in porch was another porch that was screened.

"This is a huge house," she thought aloud.

"Daddy built it to raise lots of babies, but Mommy died," Jenny told her sadly.

To change the subject Mariah asked her to show her where the bathroom was.

"I hate getting my hair washed!" exclaimed Jenny.

"Do you hate getting your hair wet or getting water in your eyes?" asked Mariah, already knowing the answer to the question.

"I guess getting the water in my eyes," admitted Jenny.

"Well, I was the same way when I was little, and I know exactly how you feel. And, I know how to fix it," Mariah said but stopped dead in her tracks as she entered the main bathroom. It was filthy and the tub was covered with soap scum and mold. She cleaned out the sink and cleared the counter and laid Jenny down on her back with her head over the sink. She gave Jenny a washcloth to cover her eyes and quickly washed her hair.

"How's that?" asked Mariah.

"It isn't so bad," Jenny said delighted. She lay very still as Mariah rinsed her long blond hair.

"Next the bath," Mariah said as she put Jenny's hair up in a towel. She scrubbed out the bathtub and bathed Jenny.

Next, she went to comb Jenny's hair, which tangled instantly. Once she finally got the tangles out, she grabbed the scissors in a drawer and cut the very bottom of her hair off to even it up and explained to Jenny that it would help it from tangling. After her hair was fully blown dry, Mariah placed the ribbon in her hair. Jenny stood on the counter and investigated the mirror and smiled and turned and threw her arms around Mariah.

"We better get you dressed," Mariah said, hugging Jenny back.

Just then they heard Cass walking down the stairs. He was already dressed in the white shirt Mariah had ironed and was putting on his suit coat.

"Don't come in yet, Daddy, I have a surprise for you!" yelled Jenny, jumping out at him.

"Jenny, you look beautiful," Cass said to his daughter with no trace of the gruffness Mariah had heard the night before.

"Daddy, you look beautiful, too!" exclaimed Jenny. Mariah had to laugh at that but stopped when her eyes met his. His cold stare was not at all like the gentle person she had heard only moments ago. His icy stare unsettled her.

"Anyone home?" yelled Doc as he entered the front door. He stood shocked in the dining room when they all came walking in.

"Wow, Jenny, you are as gorgeous as your mother. Cass, you clean up pretty good, too," he said glancing away from Jenny. "Mariah, your first success! How did you get Jenny to let you wash her hair?"

"Yes, she made it, so no water got into my eyes. It didn't even hurt when she combed it and she cut the ends off," Jenny said, twirling around, showing off her even cut.

"You cut her hair?" Cass yelled angrily, ruining the moment of triumph for Mariah. "I did not tell you that you could do that."

"Oh, Daddy I love it. It doesn't hurt to comb it anymore.

You need your hair cut, too," she said, shaking her little index finger at him with her other hand on her hip.

A smile crossed the big man's face and he picked his child up and hugged her. Jenny laughed and squealed with delight.

"We'll be back late," Cass said sternly, not looking at her. "Do what you can." Then he shot her a cold look and Mariah sensed a warning in it.

"Oh, Mariah, here are some sweet rolls for you to munch on," said Doc. "You did good; keep up the good work." Doc reached over and gave her an encouraging pat on the hand.

"Wolf, stay," Cass commanded of the dog and they were gone.

It was just her and Wolf. Everywhere she went in the house Wolf followed her. When they were in a room, he never took his eyes off her. It was making her nervous, so she started talking to him.

"Wolf, I haven't taken a bath in three days." She decided a shower was the first thing on her agenda and a thorough cleaning of that dirty room.

CHAPTER SIX

It took most of the morning to clean the bathroom and kitchen. She felt like she had done about a hundred loads of wash, including sheets for Jenny's bed. By noon she had finished Jenny's room, so she sat down and had a couple of sweet rolls and gave one to Wolf.

"OK, Wolf, we're energized again so let's put all the laundry away and then tackle the rest of the downstairs." While she was putting things away in Cass's room, she noticed several family pictures. They were a handsome bunch, even Cass, who didn't have a beard in the pictures. Cass's father passed his large size on to his sons, and their mother appeared tiny and frail looking. Other's pictures showed the brothers and wives and all the little boys in the family. There was a wedding picture of Cass and his wife. Mariah was amazed by how much Jenny looked like her. She was a beautiful woman.

She pulled the door shut on her way out and thought what a strange man Cass was. He didn't seem to know how much he had. He should be grateful and not so mean.

The rest of the day seemed to fly by as she finished cleaning the kitchen and dining room. As the sun started going down, she surveyed everything she had accomplished and was proud of herself. In fact, she had changed the downstairs of this house from a huge mess to a beautiful, livable home in one day. To celebrate, she took the rest of the sweet rolls to the back porch and watched the sun set. This was certainly the most beautiful place she had ever been. She thought to herself how life had led her to this place, and she was happy as she stared at the lake and all the green trees.

Cass was ready to leave the gathering after the funeral. He had been answering questions all day brought on by his daughter's well-groomed hair and clothes. His mother went on and on about what a find this Mariah was and how good it would be for Jenny. She wanted to meet her.

The funeral brought the whole family and town together to pay their respects to Uncle Jeb. Henry Hart was devastated by his brother's death. It was the first time Cass had seen his father cry. Cass's mom cried and he was afraid to talk to her because it just made her cry harder. Yes, old Jeb would be greatly missed. But Jenny was helping to ease the pain for everyone. Cass looked at his daughter perched on her grandpa's lap. She was making him laugh. He smiled to himself. She looked so much like her mother it made Cass's heart skip a beat and he quickly looked at the floor as tears started to surface.

"A penny for your thoughts, Cass," Doc said, catching Cass off guard.

"Are you ready to go, Doc?" asked Cass as he undid his tie.

"Yeah, you know Cub is here. I asked him why he would send Mariah out to your house on foot with a big cat prowling around," Doc said, then stopped. He had found his friend in another world, probably thinking about Becky. His heart ached for him, but he didn't want him to know he saw the lonesomeness in his face.

"God, I hate it when you do that, Doc. You start saying something and stop in the middle of a sentence," Cass said, clearly irritated.

"Well, Cub said she didn't have to worry because she was the wind that came to steal the breath from the Nakano," Doc chuckled as he said it, hoping to lighten Cass's heart.

It worked. Cass laughed with him and said, "She probably doesn't even know how to shoot a gun nor ever seen a mountain lion. I doubt if she knows how to do much of anything. She looks like she is a little wet behind the ears about everything," Cass said, quickly changing the subject. "Doc, some of the local guys are talking about tracking down the cat. I am afraid that someone is going to get hurt."

"Yeah, someone is bound to," said Doc, then he added, "Don't ruin Mariah from staying. Be pleasant. I know that is a lot to ask but do it for Jenny. You don't have to marry her, just let her take care of Jenny. Will you do that for me, Cass?"

"Now how did we get on her again?" asked Cass, "I thought we were talking about the cat?"

"I know. I have lived here long enough to believe some of what Cub's great-grandmother says. Remember she told your Dad years ago the spirits would bring him six sons of great size? They would populate the valley and unite the community. She was right. She said your Uncle Jeb would never marry and would meet his fate near dusk. She was right. She was also right when she told you and Becky, you would have a little girl. And she said a flower would be buried but the tiny seed would flourish," Doc reminded Cass.

"Let's not talk about it anymore," Cass said, clearly irritated with the conversation. He didn't want to remember the old woman's warning to him only a day before they had found out that Becky was pregnant.

Dusk had come and the rumbling in the cat's stomach prompted it to arise from a long sleep and begin yet another quest for food. It roamed down to the water's edge. The cat's keen sense of smell detected something unnerving. It sensed danger and before it finished drinking it sprang up and ran into the cover of the trees.

The cat had traveled some distance when the scent of food caught in its nostrils. Slowly and cautiously it crept toward the smell, all senses alert.

In a small clearing, an old pickup was parked, hidden from the world. The young couple in the back of the truck was engrossed in each other and oblivious to the world around them. They were naked and experiencing each other for the first time. Finally, Johnny rolled over and came to his senses and said, "Carrie, I have to get you home. Your dad is going to kill me. I love you, Carrie," he said slowly, not wanting to move, but he did slowly.

"Johnny, please not yet. Just hold me for a little while," Carrie pleaded.

"No, Carrie, we don't have time," he said as he pulled on his pants and jumped out of the back of the truck.

He was all dressed and ready to start the truck. "Come on, Carrie, don't be mad at me. Please get dressed and on the way home we'll plan when we can see each other again." Johnny looked out the back window just in time to see Carrie's perfect silhouette bending down to get her clothes, waving back at him. Within that moment all time stood still as Johnny saw the white cat pounce on the naked girl.

"God, no! Oh, God, no!" he screamed and grabbed his father's gun from the back-window gun rack. He jumped out of the truck, yelling, "Get away from her! You white son of a bitch!" He shot the gun, grazing the cat enough to scare it off. He continued to shoot wildly until all the shells were gone, even after the cat had run off. Only then did he turn his attention to Carrie and see how badly she was hurt. Her whole left shoulder was laid wide open and bleeding profusely. She was unconscious, but alive. Johnny wrapped her clothes around the wound, trying to stop the flow of blood. The closest place was Cass Hart's house and Doc might happen to be there.

The big cat was panicked and confused. It ran through the thick undergrowth until it found a high ledge. It jumped up on the ledge and hid back behind the shadows. Here, concealed by the ledge, it licked the bright red area where the bullet had grazed its shoulder. The cat's saliva would act as a natural clotting agent to stop the flow of blood and promote healing. He would continue the hunt later, the familiar taste of man still in his mouth.

CHAPTER SEVEN

C ass left his father's house late. It had been a long day and he was glad it was over. He looked over at Jenny sleeping in Doc's lap. "I can't believe the food my mother sent home with me. She was sure worried about Mariah having something to eat, wasn't she?"

"Well, Cass, if you remember the only food, except cereal, in the house were the sweet rolls I brought this morning. Tomorrow you need to go grocery shopping. Take her and Jenny to church and then go buy some food," Doc chuckled.

"I'll bet she didn't do enough today to earn her keep," Cass said as he turned into the driveway. "Since you're staying the night you can see for yourself. I'd be surprised if she even did the dishes."

Mariah felt the nudge of Wolf's nose and heard Cass's truck in the driveway. She must have drifted off to sleep. The last thing she remembered was the sun sinking behind the trees. She walked into the kitchen just in time to see Cass and Doc walk through the front door. Both stopped short in their tracks. Cass glanced around at the clean house but said nothing about it. Instead he tossed the large basket of food on the dining room table and said, "Here, my mother sent this food home. After you eat something, put it away. Doc is staying all night, so you can sleep upstairs in one of the bedrooms." Then he took Jenny, who was still lying in Doc's arms, to her bedroom and put her to bed. He noticed how clean Jenny's room was and that clean sheets were on her bed.

After Cass was gone Doc turned to Mariah and whistled,

"You have worked wonders on the house, especially this floor. It must have taken you all day and you're probably starved and exhausted. Here, sit and eat something."

Mariah uncovered the basket of goodies and took out a large sandwich. As she devoured the sandwich, Doc walked through the rest of the downstairs, complimenting her each time he went into another room. "Cass, did you get Jenny to bed?" Doc asked as he started to walk into Jenny's room.

"Yeah, I got her down," Cass replied, shutting the door but not before Doc was able to see how great Jenny's room looked.

"Cass, you ought to see the rest of the downstairs. It is spotless. Looks like Mariah is quite the worker," Doc said laughing. "I think she's going to work out just fine for you."

"You better call the sheriff and tell him you're staying here tonight in case someone needs you," Cass said, changing the subject.

Mariah had finished eating all she wanted and was putting the rest of the food away when Cass walked into the dining room. He sat down to remove his shoes and glanced up to see Mariah bending down, putting the food away. He couldn't seem to tear his eyes away as he noticed the tightness of her jeans and the roundness of her hips. It angered him when this aroused him. It had been a while since he had stopped into town and spent some time with Liz, the bartender at McCain's Tap. She was no beauty but always was available with no strings attached, no pain of a relationship.

Doc finished his phone call and caught Cass staring at Mariah. Doc smiled but knew better than to say anything. Cass saw him grinning before he could stop and said angrily, "Go to hell, Doc!" Cass picked up his shoes and stomped up to his room to change his clothes.

Wolf was at Mariah's side the whole time she was in the kitchen. She gave him a couple pieces of meat. Suddenly he started growling and pacing.

"Wolf, what is it?" asked Mariah when he started barking. "Doc, what is the matter with him?"

"I think we are about to get company," Doc said looking out the window and watching the headlights pull in. He went to the front door and opened it.

Cass came quickly out of his room ran down the stairs, clad only in a pair of jeans. Mariah would have had to be blind not to notice the large, muscular chest. She gasped and looked quickly away but not before Cass noticed.

"Who is it? They are driving extremely fast," Cass said as his feet hit the bottom stair.

Just then Johnny came bursting up the front steps and through the open the door.

"Doc! Doc! Help!" Johnny shouted, grabbing Doc and practically dragging him out to his truck.

"Good Lord, Johnny, what happened? Mariah quick, go get a blanket. Cass, my bag is in your truck. Bring it in the house. OK, Johnny let's get her in the house," Doc shouted the orders out when he saw the severity of the situation. Doc and Johnny carefully lifted Carrie out of the truck and Mariah slipped the blanket over the young girl's naked body.

After getting Carrie in the house they laid her down on the large wooden dining room table.

"Cass, better take Mariah out of the room," Doc said

"No!" Mariah was firm. "I can help. I worked three years in a hospital. I took care of my mother for two years with terminal cancer. I can help." She surprised both men with her aggressive remark.

"OK, find me some clean sheets, scissors, and boil some water," Doc said to her.

Mariah quickly complied. While Doc was preparing to sew the gaping wound and stop the bleeding in Carrie's shoulder he said, "This was the white cat, wasn't it, Johnny?"

"Yes! It happened so fast and I can't believe that damn cat jumped her while she was standing in the back of the pickup.

Is she going to die, Doc?" Johnny asked with tears streaming down his face.

Doc patted him on the shoulder. He wanted to ask him what she was doing in the back of the pickup without any clothes on, but it would have not been a good time. He had brought Carrie into this world and could not believe she was old enough to be with Johnny. Doc knew her parents probably didn't know she was with him. This would complicate things. Doc also knew how hot-headed Carrie's father, Tom Abbott, could be. Doc attempted to console Johnny, "She's lost a lot of blood and she is pretty weak. But she is young and strong, and you did the right thing by getting here fast. Cass better go get a shirt on and go get her folks. I think you better go with him, Johnny."

Cass shot Doc a look of understanding and knew that Doc didn't know if the girl was going to live or die and he needed space to work.

"Come on, Johnny," Cass said, patting him on the back and directing him out the door.

"Good God, Cass. If she dies, I will never forgive myself," moaned Johnny. "Her dad has forbidden me to see her. He's going to kill me. One minute she was in my arms and the next minute. Oh, God, what am I going to do?" Johnny started sobbing and covered his face with his hands.

"You can tell me on the way exactly what happened," Cass said, trying to show compassion, but was really thinking of his own daughter, who someday might be faced with someone like Johnny. He could see Tom Abbott's anger already and knew this might not go very well.

Doc quickly placed an IV in Carrie's arm and when he was sure she was stable he started to close the large wound. "She is starting to wake a little. I need to give her some medicine through her IV," he told Mariah, trying to finish the stitch he was doing.

"I can give it," Mariah said. "Just tell me what and how much. I did this often for Mom toward the end."

Doc nodded and returned to his stitching. He watched her skills at measuring the drug in the syringe and shooting it into the tubing. "I can see that you must have done that many times before. Good job," Doc said and made a mental note that if Cass did run her off, he could use her. Heck, he would even let her stay with him in his extra bedroom. He really wanted this to work out for Cass, so he refrained from saying anything to her about it.

"Look what we are doing to your clean floor," Doc said to Mariah, looking down at the floor where there were spots of blood everywhere.

"That's OK," smiled Mariah as she wiped Doc's brow. "It can easily be cleaned again."

They continued to work silently on the young girl. Doc put the final stitch in and checked her breathing and pulse. He determined she had a good chance.

Meanwhile, the large white cat cleaned its wound and again began its search for food. It crossed the valley as silently as a ghost. Along the way it deposited fresh spoor. It had not detected any of its own kind around, but this would warn intruders.

The cat roamed the valley until it detected a small herd of cattle. He quickly stalked a small calf, and with one mighty leap landed on its back and pulled it down easily. The cat's wounded shoulder and the earlier nights happening made him cautious and nervous, so it dragged the calf deep into the undergrowth. After being sure it was safe, he tore the carcass open and ate as much as he could. The cat covered the remains for later and again licked its wound and cleansed itself from the meal. It then returned to the rocky ledge for a nap, concealed again so nothing could detect it.

CHAPTER EIGHT

Cass didn't look forward to explaining to Tom Abbott about his daughter and Johnny's escapade. He tried to think about if it had been his daughter in this case and had to take a deep breath and concentrate on driving. He gripped the stirring wheel harder. He didn't know what to say to Johnny, who sat in the passenger side sobbing.

Tom Abbott was standing with his hands on his hips when Cass drove into the driveway. He was a large-framed man who had a great muscle mass due to logging most of his life. Cass had a feeling he would be in trouble if Tom decided to kick the shit out of Johnny.

"Tom," Cass greeted his longtime acquaintance.

"Cass," Tom looked past Cass to Johnny sitting on the passenger side. "You wouldn't happen to know where my daughter is would you, Johnny?" Tom was quite aware that Johnny looked very frightened.

"Tom," Cass said firmly, "Get Martha and come over to my house. Carrie has been hurt. Doc is working on her now."

Tom's face grew very angry. "Goddamn! You wrecked that pickup and she got hurt, didn't you?" Tom shouted at Johnny, reaching across Cass.

Cass grabbed his arm and stated more firmly, "Tom, there was no wreck. Go get your wife and come to my house." He looked deep into Tom's eyes and saw Tom's anger turn into fear. Tom turned and went into the house to get his wife. Within a couple of minutes, they ran out of the house and jumped into their car and followed Cass to his house.

Doc met them at the porch and prepared them before they entered the house. "She's stable and resting well. She should stay here tonight so I can watch her. I think she will come out of this OK. Johnny did the right thing bringing her here," Doc said, helping Martha in the door.

As they entered the house Johnny told them the story of the attack of the white cat, leaving out a few of the details—especially what he and Carrie had been doing.

"God damn you! You were not supposed to see her!" yelled Tom grabbing for him. Tom again was stopped short by Cass's big arm.

"Don't do it, Tom. Go and see your daughter," Cass said firmly, although if it was his daughter the boy would be bloody, he thought.

Mariah, who had been hanging back in the shadows of the darkened living room, came out when she heard the commotion. "Please, remember Jenny is sleeping." she said. Everyone turned and stared at her. Finally, Doc broke the silence and introduced Mariah as Jenny's nanny and explained what a great help she had been to him with Carrie. Then he spoke to the Abbotts.

"She suffered numerous large gashes on her shoulder. I don't think there will be any permanent damage, except for scars, but it's going to be a long recovery. I have sedated her, and this should last most of the night."

"Johnny, why don't you go on home? Your parents are probably worried sick about you," said Cass, knowing his presence was causing friction.

"Yeah, I haven't had time to call them. But I'll come by in the morning to see Carrie," Johnny said, touching her hair.

"Oh, no you won't!" yelled Tom going for Johnny again. Cass stepped in again and Martha surprised them all by gently saying, "Go home, Johnny. I'll call you in the morning and tell you how she's doing. Don't come over in the morning. Let her heal."

Johnny nodded and slowly left the house, looking back at Carrie one more time. They moved Carrie to the couch and Tom and Martha stayed in the recliners to be near her. Mariah followed Doc and Cass up the stairs and Wolf followed. Mariah was surprised to see that there were four more bedrooms upstairs besides Jennie's bedroom downstairs. Wolf followed Cass like a loyal companion.

Mariah fell on top of the unmade bed, exhausted. She hoped she would be able to start on the upstairs cleaning tomorrow. Her first day on her new job was finally over and quite an exciting day it had been. She slowly put on her sleep T-shirt; lying back on the bed she fell asleep almost instantly.

The white lion awoke in the night. The gunshot that had grazed the cat was bleeding. Again, the cat licked his wound and fell asleep quickly.

CHAPTER NINE

Mariah was abruptly awakened by a hard shake on her shoulder. It was Cass. She sat straight up in bed. It was still dark.

"What's the matter? What time is it?" she asked.

"Five o'clock, time to get up. My folks will be bringing over the fixings for breakfast. Can you cook?" Cass asked. His voice was low and somewhat irritated.

"Yes, I can cook. Is Jenny up yet?" she asked.

"No, you need to get her up. Get her ready for church. Then you can cook breakfast. You'll probably have to stay with Carrie while everyone goes to church," he said and walked out the door and shut it behind him. He was angry with himself. He had stood over her a moment with the moonlight shining in before waking her. A long slim leg was on top of the covers, her long dark hair spread all over the pillow, and even though her eyes were closed he was aware of their almost loving brown color. He had to stop this kind of thinking. He went to the bathroom and took a long cool shower.

Mariah sat on the end of the bed hoping she had been covered up when he came in. She had covered up with the quilts that were on the chair after she put on her oversized T-shirt but was pretty sure she had kicked most of them off in the night. She had no idea he would be coming in to wake her up or she would have stayed in her clothes. Did he just give her about six jobs? She wiped the sleep from her eyes and got dressed. She used the downstairs bathroom to scrub her face and pull her hair back into a ponytail. She was glad Cass's folks were coming over; she was anxious to meet them.

Mariah had found some coffee yesterday in one of the cupboards and put it on to perk. The Abbotts were still sleeping but started to stir. She had instantly liked Martha Abbott and hoped she would get up soon. Mariah went to wake up Jenny before everyone started getting up.

She opened Jenny's door and gently touched her cheek. "Good morning, sweetie," Mariah said. "Did you sleep well?"

"Uh-huh," Jenny said, instantly awake and smiling.

"Jenny, we have some company. A young girl got hurt last night and she is on the couch. Her parents are sleeping in the chairs in the front room, so we need to be quiet until they get up." explained Mariah. "Your dad says you should get ready for church. What would you like to wear?"

Jenny had picked out a dress that Mariah had laundered the day before.

"Great, we'll get you dressed in a while. Let's go to the kitchen. Your grandparents are bringing over stuff to make breakfast."

Doc was up as they entered the kitchen and had already found the coffee. The few unruly gray hairs he had were sticking straight up on the top of his head. His potbelly from eating too many sweet rolls rolled over his pants. He broke into a huge grin when they walked into the room.

"Good morning, ladies," he said, leaning up against the counter, making his potbelly stick out even more.

"Too bad we don't have any sweet rolls. This coffee would taste even better with them!" he chuckled.

"Gram and Gumpa are going to bring something to eat. They always do," Jenny said. Just then the front door opened. "They're here!" she said and quickly ran to them.

A tiny gray-haired woman and an older version of Cass walked through the door.

"Good morning, Doc, and you must be Mariah," the woman said and took Mariah's hand. "My, but you are a pretty thing. Isn't she, Henry?"

"Yes, Mama, that she is. Hi, I'm Henry and this is Edna." He shook her hand then picked up Jenny. "Where is your daddy, little girl?"

"I think he is in the shower," replied Jenny, hugging her grandpa.

The Abbotts were up and walked in the kitchen and greeted the Harts. Doc checked on Carrie and gave her another sedative. She was resting quietly as he explained to the Harts what had happened.

"Mariah!" yelled Cass as he came into the room. "Why isn't Jenny dressed?"

Mariah instantly was embarrassed by his outburst and softly said, "She hasn't had her breakfast. I thought it better to dress her later so she would not drop anything on her dress."

"Get her dressed," he demanded.

Mariah lowered her head and bit her lip so she wouldn't say what she was thinking. She took Jenny and left the room without looking up at anyone.

When they left the room, Edna walked over to Cass and hit him harmlessly on the arm and said, "Cass you are going to drive her away like you did all the rest. I want you to quit being so ugly to her."

"Sorry, Mom, I just told her to get Jenny dressed. If she can't do just one simple thing maybe she isn't going to work out," he uttered, looking away.

Edna gave Cass a stern look and shook her head.

"Mariah why did Daddy yell at you?" asked Jenny as she was getting dressed.

"I don't know, baby," Mariah answered, because she didn't know either. She decided the less she had to do with that man, the easier it would be. In a few minutes Jenny was all cleaned up and dressed, looking adorable in a white lace dress. Mariah was going to have to find something to cover up the pretty dress, so she did not spill anything on it.

"OK, let's get you some food," Mariah said, dreading the thought of facing Cass again.

The men were sitting down at the large kitchen table having coffee when she walked in. Mariah avoided looking at anyone and went directly to cooking.

Martha had already started the bacon and Edna was breaking eggs in a bowl.

"Mariah don't let Cass bother you. His bark is worse than his bite," Edna said, squeezing Mariah's hand. She had said it loud enough that all in the kitchen could hear, which prompted a small laugh from Doc. This only angered his big bearded friend more, which made Doc laugh even more.

"Yes ma'am." Mariah smiled at her, knowing Cass was not going to deter her from this job, no matter what he said or did to her.

The women had set the table and placed all the food on the large dining room table. They all sat down to eat.

During breakfast Henry Hart said, "I'm raising the reward of the white cat to five thousand dollars. I have contacted a tracker by the name of Bruno Grey. He will be coming to town soon. I know we are going to have some that will be foolish and attempt to get the cat, but this has got to end. My grandchildren can't even play outside. And now what has happened to Carrie, it has to come to an end."

"We know the cat has only been on this side of the lake," Cass said. "We could form a search party."

"I saw a track on the other side of the bridge," Mariah softly stated, remembering how large the print was.

"What? When?" he yelled angrily as he looked toward Mariah.

"The day I walked out here I stopped before the bridge and walked down to the lake. I saw a huge cat print. It was bigger than my hand," Mariah said, getting ready for another insult. But instead Henry Hart came to her rescue.

"It might have crossed the bridge. Mariah, you need to show us where this track is," Henry volunteered.

"Jeb was killed on this side of the bridge. Carrie was attacked also on this side. I hardly think the cat will cross the bridge," Cass said sarcastically, looking at Mariah. "I'm sure you don't even know what a cat track looks like," he venomously added with a smart laugh.

There it is Mariah thought, well prepared this time for his hurtful words. "I can show you," she simply said. This time she looked at Cass and he looked away.

After breakfast everyone readied themselves for church while Mariah did the dishes. The Abbotts moved Carrie to their house and the Harts left for church, leaving her alone with Wolf. When everyone was gone, she took a bath and washed her hair. She busied herself with more housework until Cass and Jenny returned home.

They had just changed their clothes when Cass sternly said to her, "Let's go look at those tracks you thought you saw. When we get done, we will go get some groceries." Cass threw the truck keys to her, "Here, you drive."

Now what was he up to? "Me? Why?" asked Mariah, wondering if he was testing her to see if she could drive.

"Because you know where the tracks are, and I would like to see if you can drive the truck if you are going to be here alone with Jenny," he said, thinking she was a city girl and would probably plead with him to drive because she could not drive the straight stick. He gave one of his smirky little laughs as he turned and got into the passenger side of the truck after putting Jenny up in the seat. But she didn't complain. She climbed in the driver's side and waited for Wolf to jump up in the back of the truck.

"This ought to be good," Cass said, snickering to himself.

Mariah sat there for a while and could see that the manual transmission was just like her neighbor Randy's truck. He had taught her how to drive it two summers ago so she could haul firewood for the winter. She smiled to herself. Yes, her mother was right. She had always told her that everything you do or learn prepares you for something down the road.

"OK," Mariah said as she stepped on the clutch and shifted the truck into reverse. She slowly let out on the clutch and carefully maneuvered the big truck out of the driveway then turned it successfully around without killing it once. She turned onto the main road and went through the gears without a hitch.

Cass couldn't believe it and kept his head turned looking out the window. She had obviously done this before.

CHAPTER TEN

Mariah stopped the truck on the road where she had cut through to the lake the day she walked to Cass's house. She jumped out of the truck, ready to show him she knew what she was talking about.

"Come on, Wolf," said Cass as he picked up Jenny. Mariah led them down to the water's edge and after only a couple of minutes she found the tracks. "There, see, it's bigger than my hand." She bent down and put her hand over the print.

"Cass, there are more, and they weren't here before," she said, pointing down the shoreline.

Cass saw the size of the print and could tell the old prints and the new prints were the same cat. Thinking out loud he said, "It crossed the bridge. Carrie got hurt about eight o'clock last night five miles from here. These prints are surely fresh from early this morning. This is only four miles from town." Cass looked across the lake and shook his head in disbelief. "Let's go to town. You can get the groceries—you know what kind of stuff to buy. Drop me off at McCain's; I need some help with this."

When they pulled up to McCain's Tap, Cass said, "I'll take Jenny and Wolf with me. You go on over to the store for groceries and come back here to pick us up. Tell Ted, the owner, to make a ticket and I'll be in to pay it at the end of the week."

Mariah found the little grocery store had everything she needed. She spent quite a bit of time because they needed just about everything. When she got to the checkout she asked for Ted.

"He is not here. He had to go home for a while," a young man said.

"I'm buying these groceries for Cass Hart. He said to have Ted put it on a ticket," Mariah said, getting a little nervous. "He is in McCain's Tap. Please call him there and he will tell you."

"No, that's OK. I've heard about you. You're Cass's daughter's nanny. No problem. My name is Larry. You're Mariah, right?" he said as he started working on the groceries.

"Yes, nice to meet you," Mariah replied with a smile.

They put the groceries in the back of the truck and Mariah thought to herself. The small town had already spread the news of her arrival. Just like home, she thought. Some things never change.

Mariah walked into McCain's and found Cass and Jenny sitting at a table with four other men. She felt a little out of place but pulled up a chair alongside of Jenny. All the men were staring at her, but Cass didn't introduce her to them. She looked up to see a familiar face walk in. It was Cub. He walked over to her and pulled up a chair.

"I have fifty dollars for you," he said and handed her the money.

"What is this for?" she asked, surprised.

"I sold some of your car parts. Not much, but more than you had," he said, and a smile crossed his handsome face.

"Thanks, Cub," Mariah said.

Cass had called Cub to come to McCain's. "Thanks for coming, Cub. Can you look at some tracks for me? The white cat injured the Abbott girl on the south side of the lake and I just saw tracks this side of the bridge."

"Yes, I will look at them for you," Cub answered.

Mariah could see Cub thought a lot of Cass. They shook hands and Cub agreed to be at Cass's house at seven the next morning.

Behind her Mariah heard a rough female voice yell, "I don't know why you have anything to do with that damn Indian."

The woman walked over to Cass, threw her head back, and laughed and winked at him. Soon the woman was standing next to her. The woman had dark auburn hair, a very large bosom that spilled from the top of her blouse and was dressed in a very short miniskirt. Mariah had never been so close to anyone that had so much makeup on. She could not help but stare.

"Well now, who do we have here?" she asked, looking at Mariah.

"This is Mariah," Cass quietly said, "Jenny's nanny."

"Nanny, huh? Right! Sure Cass," she threw back her head again and did another deep laugh. "Hi ya, Mariah. I'm Liz." She laughed again and winked at Cass. The men at the table laughed but abruptly stopped when Cass glared at them.

"Let's go," he said to Mariah as he picked up Jenny and stood to leave. "See you at my house at seven, Cub. And any of you that would like to see the prints." He walked out with Mariah behind him. She said goodbye to the table of men and was curious to why they were suddenly leaving.

"I'll drive," he said, getting in the driver's side.

When they got in the truck Mariah said, "I would like to go to church next Sunday. Would that be OK?"

It took Cass a few seconds to respond. He was thinking of her walking in with the family. Already people had the idea they were together. He would not be able to go into McCain's without someone teasing him about it now. "Yeah, OK," he finally responded. He would just have to set people straight. He had no intention of ever getting involved with anyone again. It hurt too bad.

It took a long time to put the groceries away. Mariah found both Cass and Jenny taking a nap in the front room when she was done. She went to the back porch and sat watching the lake. It was mid spring and the foliage was many colors of green. The forest across the lake was getting thick. The mountains above the forest still had lots of snow on them and it would continue to melt and feed the lake. Looking across the glass water she could see a pontoon boat making its way down the lake. It looked like a whole family was aboard. When it got to Cass's dock, she recognized the family as one of Cass's brother's family. The man looked a lot like Cass but without a beard. The woman was as tall as Mariah but older. There were four little boys she would later find out ranged from the age of one to twelve.

They walked through the backyard and into the back porch where Mariah sat.

"Hi," she said when they entered the door.

"You must be Mariah," the woman said with a smile. "I am Judy. This is my husband Gus and my kids Kevin, Kurt, Kent, and little Kenny. We tried to phone earlier but no one was home. Where is my favorite brother-in-law?" she said as she reached for Mariah's hand.

"He is in the front room with Jenny taking a nap," Mariah said, smiling.

"Come on guys, let's attack Uncle Cass," said Kevin, the oldest boy. They all went running except Judy and little Kenny. Mariah offered Judy a seat and they sat until Gus came out and said, "We better head home before dark." He was carrying a handgun.

"What is that?" Judy demanded.

"I borrowed it from Cass's gun cabinet until tomorrow. I don't want to be without protection; we will talk about it later." He gave her a weak smile and put the gun in his pocket.

Judy knew that look and it alarmed her. "Make sure the boys don't get it. What are you afraid of? Do you think the cat will swim the lake after us?" she said joking but stopped short when he did not joke back. "OK," she said, "Let's not take any chances."

Cass walked to the boat with them, Jenny on his shoulders. Mariah walked partway to the dock and gave a wave goodbye.

"It's getting dark. Get in the house," he ordered Mariah.

"The cat will be prowling tonight, and you would be fair game standing out here."

He had again caught her off guard with his abrupt order. Angrily she turned and walked into the house, ready to snap back at him, but she didn't.

He slowed his gait to watch her walk into the house. He watched the way her hips swayed and something deep inside him stirred. He came into the kitchen and gave her an icy stare, hoping to hide whatever it was that was happening to him. "I'm locking the doors. We will have company early in the morning. Everyone is meeting here to track the white lion. You will watch Jenny tomorrow and you will not go out of the house," he demanded.

Mariah sighed. Is this the way he is going to treat me? Like a slave or a piece of dirt? It seemed he enjoyed making her feel inferior. She knew very little about men and had never been in a relationship. Twenty-four years old and she was still a virgin. Most women had been married and had kids by this age. Mariah's life had not allowed her to find anyone yet to show her the passion of life. She was not prepared for a man like Cass Hart. She wanted him to be nicer to her. Everyone else treated her great, why didn't he like her? She stared at him as he played with Jenny. She turned red when he caught her staring and she went upstairs so she did not have to look at him. Even the way he looked at her made her feel inferior. Why, she thought?

CHAPTER ELEVEN

Mariah was awakened abruptly the next morning with a shake on her shoulder. She opened her eyes to see Cass towering above her again.

"Get up. The men will be here shortly. Make some coffee and pack me something to eat," he growled and walked out of the room.

"I have got to get me an alarm clock," Mariah thought out loud. She washed her face and pulled her hair back into a ponytail. She wondered if this would be the day the white lion would be found. Last night she had overheard Cass tell Gus confirming they hired the man named Bruno Grey; he goes by his last name Grey. He was a famous great tracker and hunter. His dogs were known to find lost travelers and even lost children. He had never lost a dog.

She went into the kitchen and made coffee. Cass had unloaded most of his guns from the gun cabinet and had them cleaned and laid out on the kitchen table. He must have gotten up early, she thought. He looked extremely cranky this morning.

Cass was very aware she was looking at him and he was not about to talk to her if he didn't have to. He stood over her bed before he woke her again this morning. She was almost fully uncovered and clad only in bikini panties and an oversized T-shirt. He had resisted the strong urge to touch her. It angered him even more that he could almost not control himself.

"Would you like some coffee?" Mariah asked as she carried a cup to the table for him and sat it down.

"God dammit!" Cass grumbled, hoping the tone would mask his thoughts. "Move it to the other side."

"Sure," Mariah sighed and moved the coffee. She went back to fixing him something to eat, thinking he could get his own coffee the next time. It didn't work trying to be nice to him.

Wolf started pacing the floor and growled a low growl, but his tail was wagging. Cass walked to the door and opened it.

"Cub come on in," Cass said warmly.

Cub smiled when he saw Mariah. "Good morning, Mariah." Mariah returned his friendly greeting.

"Cass, it is snowing in the mountains and will be raining here before too long," Cub said as he sat down at the large kitchen table.

"Did you look at the tracks?" Cass questioned.

"Yes, they are from the same cat. It is not unusual for a cat to travel many miles searching for food," Cub informed Cass.

"Where would you say this cat is now, Cub? Where would you look?"

Cub looked at his friend and shook his head, "He could be anywhere in the valley. You will not find him unless he finds you."

"Bruno Grey is bringing his dogs. They will track him. Then we will shoot him," Cass assured him.

"No, my friend. He will live to kill again. Great-grandmother says this. Not enough blood has been shed. The cat will kill again," Cub said but stopped when there was a knock at the door and a growl and barking from Wolf.

Cass opened the door and Wolf continued to growl as the man entered and Mariah couldn't help but stare at the filthy, longhaired man. He stood less than six foot, thin, and probably in his forties. Mariah was sure he hadn't bathed for weeks when she got a whiff of him. Wolf snarled and Cass made him go lie down.

The man looked at Mariah and smiled a toothless grin. "Mornin' ma'am," he said, looking her up and down.

Mariah shuddered but smiled weakly. It was very unsettling to her that the man continued to stare at her through the conversation with Cass. Cass was more than aware of the man's interest in Mariah. He attempted many times to get Grey to look at him in the conversation but had failed. Maybe it had been a mistake to bring Grey into the small valley. Could he trust Grey with the women of the Elk Lake? Cub also had become aware of the man's stare.

Finally, without looking at Cub, Grey asked Cass, "Is this damn Indian going with us?"

"No," answered Cass.

"Good, good. Hate to waste a good shell," he chuckled. "Cass, you have a beautiful wife," Grey said as he scratched and rearranged his crotch.

"She's not my wife," Cass said, getting up from the table. "Mariah, got my lunch packed?"

"Oh, don't have to buy the cow, the milk is free?" Grey said laughing while he watched Mariah's face turn red.

"Grey, don't ever talk like that again in my house," Cass said in a low warning tone, which was enough for Grey to move his gaze to Cass's face, then to the dark slants of Cub's eyes.

Grey got up from his chair, tipped his hat to Mariah, and went outside much to Mariah's relief. His stench remained in the room for a while.

The telephone rang and it was Doc. Cass informed Mariah, "Doc will pick you and Jenny up in about an hour. He needs to go check on Carrie and he would like your help," Cass said as he moved to the window and verified that all the men were there and ready to go.

"I will help you load your guns in the truck and will talk to you when you return. Be careful," Cub said to Cass, then turned and said to Mariah, "Mariah, don't ever let that man in here when Cass is not here. Understand me?" He smiled when Mariah nodded her head yes. He looked at Cass and didn't have to say anything but nod. Both men walked out the door looking at each other, but no other words were exchanged in the house.

Cass returned to the house only minutes later. Mariah was crying. "What's the matter?" he asked her.

Drying her tears, she said, "I have never seen anyone as scary as him. His stare was unbearable." She shuddered.

"Don't ever let him in the house when I am not here. Don't ever open the door. Don't go anywhere unless you have Wolf with you. Wolf, stay," he ordered. "Thank God Jenny wasn't up yet. Tell her I will see her tonight."

This was a totally different Cass, she thought. She really didn't understand men, she said to herself.

The cat feasted on the remains of its kill, finishing all of it. With its belly full, it set out for shelter. Sniffing the air, he knew it would soon be raining. He walked through the dense forest, moving quietly through the undercover. Even though the cat was more than nine feet from nose to tip of its tail and weighted over two hundred pounds, the animal hardly made a sound. Soon it found shelter under a protruding ledge where it curled up to sleep and stay out of the rain.

Mariah and Jenny waited on the front porch for Doc. Wolf's ears perked up long before Doc's old station wagon turned in the drive. Wolf didn't growl but started wagging his tail, as the familiar car came to a stop.

"Good morning, ladies!" shouted Doc, "Jump in."

Mariah quickly loaded Jenny and put Wolf in the back before she got in. They reached the Abbott's house shortly and were warmly welcomed by Martha Abbott. Carrie was up, sitting in a chair. She looked pale but smiled widely as they entered.

"How are you doing, Carrie?" asked Doc, "This is Mariah. She's the one who helped me fix you up the other night."

"Hi, thank you," Carrie said, shaking Mariah's hand.

Carrie was a beautiful girl, Mariah thought. Her almond shaped eyes and white, flawless skin highlighted by her light auburn hair made her stunning. Mariah wondered how old she was.

"Come with me, Jenny, let's go get some cookies," Martha said, taking the child out of the room until they finished.

"Now, let's check on that wound," Doc said. He yelled out to Martha in the next room while removing the bandages, "Looks good, Martha, no signs of infection. I will give her another shot of antibiotics. You've done a good job of keeping it clean and dry."

"Johnny went with them to hunt the lion," Carrie offered in conversation. "Hope he will be all right. Pa sure hates him."

"Did your dad go too?" asked Doc.

"Yeah, that's what worries me."

"Carrie, are you sixteen yet?" asked Doc.

"Yes, almost seventeen," she answered.

Doc lowered his voice so Martha could not hear and asked, "Are you and Johnny sexually active?"

The young girl's face turned red and she shook her head yes.

"Please promise me we will talk about that at another time before you do it again. I do not want you getting pregnant." Doc winked at her. "Now squeeze my fingers as hard as you can. That's good, good. Carrie, you are very lucky. You are going to have some scars, but no permanent damage. I'll come again tomorrow and change the bandage again. We have to be extremely careful of infection."

Martha teared up as she shook Doc's hand as they left.

"Thanks, Doc and please come and visit me again, Mariah." Mariah shook her head yes and hugged the small, stout woman. She must have looked a lot like Carrie when she was younger.

Mariah and Jenny rode with Doc while he did some of his rounds. He had a small office in town where he saw patients on Tuesdays and Thursdays, but he liked to visit his older and more bedridden patients on his days out of the office.

"Let me buy you lunch," Doc said to Mariah and Jenny.

"Oh, please say yes Mariah!" begged Jenny. "Then I can have some ice cream."

"OK," Mariah agreed.

They walked into McCain's Tap, which was the only place in town to eat. When they sat down Doc said, "Everyone must be hunting for that cat. There is no one here."

"What will it be Doc, sweetheart?" yelled Liz halfway across the room. Mariah turned to see Liz again dressed in a miniskirt and a short top that revealed the top of her ample bosom.

"We'll have the special, Liz. Doesn't look like you are very busy today," Doc commented.

"You want the special today? Meatloaf? Doc you need more variety in your life. Well, honey, you like meatloaf, too?" Liz directed the question to Mariah.

"That will be fine," Mariah answered, 'Could you bring Jenny a half order, and could you bring a bone or something for Wolf?'

"Sure, I'll bring him some scraps," she said and paraded across the room yelling, "Three McCain's specials and a plate of scraps. The damn health department doesn't make it here anyway."

"Interesting woman," Mariah said to Doc. Mariah had never seen a woman this brazen. It made her uncomfortable and she was not sure how to take Liz.

"Liz is quite the girl," Doc said winking back.

Liz quickly brought their food and pulled up a chair, "Mariah, you're the talk of the town," she blurted out.

"What do you mean?" Mariah asked, swallowing a bite.

"It's just old Cass won't be visiting here much in the future I guess."

Confused, Mariah looked at Doc to rescue her.

"Liz, watch your mouth. Jenny is here," warned Doc.

"Sorry, sorry, it's just that Cass has these needs and I know all about them," Liz directed the insult to Mariah, who didn't know how to take it, and had no idea what she was talking about.

"She knows what I am talking about," Liz crushed her cigarette out in an ashtray she grabbed from another table, giving Mariah a look of loathing, and went back into the kitchen.

"Did I do something wrong?" Mariah asked Doc.

Doc was totally convinced this little girl had not seen too many women like Liz. "Seems you are a threat to her. Don't worry, she is everyone's sweetheart."

Mariah was confused and was glad when she saw Cub walking through the door.

"Doc, Mariah, hi Jenny," Cub greeted them and pulled up a chair.

"Doc, I need you to go see my great-grandmother. She has a sore on her leg that is not healing. Her eyes are so bad she didn't realize how bad it was until today when it hurt her to walk," he explained.

"Yes, we can go see her as soon as Jenny has some ice cream," Doc said and held his arm up, waving to get Liz's attention, "Liz, bring Jenny some ice cream."

"You want something Redskin?" Liz asked Cub.

Cub ignored her and turned to Mariah, "Great Grandmother wants to meet you."

"Bringing her home to meet the family, Redskin?" Liz quipped.

"Liz, please!" Doc exclaimed.

Liz threw back her head and gave one of her laughs as she walked off, her large breasts bouncing with each step.

"Lord, that woman is unreal," Doc said.

Jenny finished her ice cream and they all climbed into Doc's station wagon and followed Cub to his great-grandmother's. They journeyed several miles out of town to the Native American reservation, then they turned off on an old dirt road. Soon they came upon about twenty small cabins that formed a small community. Doc parked the car. They all got out and walked to the first cabin. Large animal pelts were nailed to the walls and antlers and carvings set all around the small porch. Inside the tiny cabin sat Cub's great-grandmother on an old couch. Her leg was propped up on the coffee table in front of her. Cataracts covered her eyes, giving her a mystic look. Her gray hair was braided into two long braids. She was completely blind, but knew they were there, and who they were.

"Great-grandmother, Doc is here with Mariah," Cub announced.

"Yes, and Jenny and you even brought the dog, Wolf," she replied and added, "Mariah, come sit by me. We will visit."

"I will look at your leg now," Doc said to the old woman.

"Yes, please, go ahead," Nooka encouraged.

Mariah sat by the old woman and Jenny sat next to Mariah. Mariah looked at the wrinkled old woman, trying to guess just how old she was. She had never seen anyone this old.

"I have met you many times in my dreams. Although my sight has been robbed from me, I am still able to see things in my dreams. The Great Spirit put this inside me. The white people say it is a gift," she said slowly and squeezed Mariah's hand. "Has the Nakano visited you in your dreams yet?'

"Ma'am?" questioned Mariah. She was not sure what she meant.

"Have you dreamed of the white lion yet?

"No, I have not dreamed of a lion." She glanced at Doc while he tended Nooka's leg. He shrugged his shoulders and didn't say anything.

"You will. Do not let it frighten you. The Nakano is as old as the valley. It came once in my life to me. I was the wind that took its breath. Now I am too old. I will help you like the old shaman helped me before." The old one said as she shifted her leg when Doc poured medicine on the open area.

Jenny had gone to sleep and lay peacefully on the end of the old couch. Doc finished bandaging the old woman's leg. Cub and Doc walked outside per the request from Nooka so she could talk to Mariah.

"Today they hunt the spirit cat but will not be able to find him. It has not killed enough yet. The only one that can kill it or find it is you. It will be drawn to you. But do not worry. It will not kill you. It is curious of you but also fears you." The old woman went on slowly to say, "When you first see it, look deep in its eyes; then it will know who you are. At night you will dream about it and it will dream of you. When it comes time to send the Nakano back to the mountain, you will know. Anytime you have a dream you need to tell me, and I will translate it for you. Anytime you need to talk I will listen. No one will believe or understand. I know right now you are wondering if I am crazy or not, right?" asked the old woman as she patted Mariah's hand.

"With all due respect, ma'am, do you know I am just a nanny for Jenny here? I have no powers. I am from Kansas and never been to the state of Washington before. I think you have got me mixed up with someone else," Mariah politely told her.

"I know where you came from. I have seen you caring for your mother for years. Time will make you a believer. Slowly you will believe. I remember when I did not believe. Now take the sleeping child home and come see me when you have your first dream. Come share that with me and I will tell you what the white lion will do next." The old woman abruptly brought the conversation to an end.

Mariah gently picked up Jenny and walked out the door and stood on the front porch. It had just started to rain. "She thinks I am some chosen one," she said to Doc and Cub, shaking her head.

Both men smiled at her, knowing the predictions of the old woman in the past were always close to being true.

"We better get you two home," Doc said, "This rain will put a halt to any hunting or tracking of the big cat. Cub make sure your great-grandmother takes that medicine I left. Let me know if she doesn't."

"Thanks, Doc," Cub said, shaking Doc's hand. "Mariah, come back and see my great-grandmother again soon," he encouraged, smiling down at her.

"I will," Mariah said, "What is her name?"

"Nooka. It means the wind," he answered.

CHAPTER TWELVE

All the men called it quits when it started pouring rain. They found the tracks at the lake's edge and there the dogs picked up the trail but lost it at the south side of the bridge where the cat had attacked Carrie. Then it started to rain. Tired, and wet, most of them ended up at McCain's to have a few brandies to warm up. Sitting around a large table were Cass, his brothers, Henry Hart, and Tom Abbott.

The tracker Grey had spotted Liz and was buying her drinks. They also sat around a large round table along with some of the other men that had been on the hunt.

"So, you couldn't find your little kitty, huh, gentlemen?" taunted Liz. "Ask old Ben over there in the corner. He'll tell you all about it. Ben is ninety-nine years old and says when he was fifteen the Nakano came down from the mountain."

Grey's eyes widened, "Really, well get him over here. I'd like to buy him a beer and hear that story."

Old Ben got up and moved slowly to the table after some coaxing from Liz. Age had bent him over and arthritis made it hard to move from one place to another, but he came into McCain's every night for a beer.

Ben sat down gingerly and began his story, "I was but fifteen. It had snowed a lot that spring in the mountains, much like this year. First thing we knew it was killin' children. Pickin' them off one at a time. It didn't care whether it was white child or an Indian child. It just killed them, and then ate them. The valley formed a search party to kill the cat. Then one of the women saw it. The woman said it was big and white and that it was the Nakano. Now the Nakano is an old Native American lore. The bad spirit takes on the body of a white mountain lion. Yep and this spirit cat was a mean one. My father and others laid traps, but it was too smart for them," stopping for a moment, old Ben took a long drink of his beer and went on. "The Native Americans told the story of years ago how even the bravest of men could not kill it. Shit, they could hardly even get a look at it. Only a woman that was the chosen one could kill it. This is a fact. I know this because I was there when she brought it back to the village. That woman was Cub's own great-grandmother, Nooka."

"Old man, that is a good story," Grey said laughing. "Now how in the hell did she kill it?"

"Don't know for sure. She just went out in the forest look-ing for her brother. She said she had dreamed the white spirit cat was going to kill her brother, so she went looking for it. It had indeed killed her brother. She found the half-eaten body of her brother and yep, the next day she came dragging the white pelt of that white lion home. Just like it rolled over and died for her. I saw it. It was as white as snow. The only black on it was the tip of its tail," the old man explained, "She still has the skin. She skinned it and treated the pelt herself."

"This I have to see!" Grey exclaimed, "Where is this old woman now?"

"Just west of town, first cabin," answered the old man.

Grey roared with laughter, "Old man, are you fooling with me?" he asked, grabbing the front of Ben's shirt.

"Grey, leave him alone," Cub calmly said from the door. He had just walked in McCain's and had heard most of Ben's story especially about his great-grandmother.

"Get over here Redskin and make me," Grey continued his hold on the old man.

Cub walked over to the table. When he did all the Harts and Tom Abbott stood and went to stand behind Cub. Cass walked up to Grey and ordered, "Let Ben go, Grey."

Grey, seeing that he was outnumbered, let the front of the frightened old man go. "Damn fairy tale," he said and patted old Ben's face. "I'll get that big cat and you will see me skin it."

Cub was staring at Grey and had a premonition that Grey would try to see the pelt. Instead of worrying about if the man would go to his great-grandmother's and harm her to see it, he offered, "I will show you the pelt."

This caught Grey off guard.

"You'll what?"

"I'll show you the pelt. Ben speaks the truth," Cub answered.

"Maybe later, Redskin; I have a lot of drinking to do. And I might add, if I can get Liz drunk enough tonight, I might have a little extracurricular activity."

"Not unless you take a bath," Liz said holding her nose.

"Would you wash my back, little lady?" asked Grey then laughed and drank his whiskey down. He then grabbed Liz and loudly asked her, "Take me to your house so I can clean up?"

"It's going to cost you," Liz joked, then both walked out the door staggering.

"Cub, you know he will try to see the pelt," Cass warned.

"Yes, I believe he will. I will warn great-grandmother." Cub walked to the door but turned before he left and added, "Thanks."

Henry Hart put his hand on Cass's shoulder and said, "Son, this Grey is an evil man. Maybe he has met his match with this cat."

Cass smiled back at his father but remembered the way Grey looked at Mariah and said, "Yeah, I don't want him around Jenny."

Changing the subject Henry said, "The church social is a week from next Sunday. I don't like the idea that all those people will be out in the middle of an open area."

"A week from this coming Sunday?" Cass's brother Mike asked, "Man, you know all the girls will need a new dress! Are we going to let them go to Everett themselves or should we take them on Saturday?"

Mike's twin brother Matt said, "Let's let them go themselves; I really don't feel like spending the whole day shopping." They all agreed with him.

Gus, who was the only one of the brothers that had met Mariah, said, "Cass, are you going to bring Mariah?" He thought twice about saying that after Cass's reaction.

"Her job is to watch Jenny, not to go on outings," Cass roared.

"True, but Jenny will be going to the social. What are you going to do, leave Mariah home?" Henry Hart asked his son jokingly. "Son, I like the girl. Are you afraid that people are going to think she is more than a friend?" Henry could read his son's face and knew that he had hit on his son's true feelings.

"Hell, I like her too, Cass. She can go with me and Judy," Gus offered.

"No!" yelled Cass and got up. "She isn't going and that is it! I'm going home," he grumbled and walked out the door.

All at the table grew silent. Henry Hart's heart warmed, and he smiled. This woman was going to be good for his son. Cass's brothers smiled at each other, all knowing what their dad was thinking and they all winked at each other. Cass's brother Matt said, "Cass thinks he is hiding his feelings." They all laughed.

"She will have to put up with a lot," Henry Hart commented, and they all laughed again.

Cass drove home in the pouring rain. As he drove in the driveway it was pleasant to see lights on in the house and Jenny standing on the porch, waving.

"Hi, daddy, did you get him?" the child asked.

Cass reached down and picked her up, "No baby, not today."

"Come on in and have piece of apple pie. I made it," she said proudly.

"Apple pie, that you made. Well, I might just have to have some," he teased.

Mariah cut a large piece of pie and gave it to Jenny to carry to the table for her dad. Her little hands almost lost it a couple of times. Her excitement was overwhelming to Cass.

"Whoa! Whoa! I've got it," he said, "You made this?"

"Yep, I helped cut the apples up and rolled out the crust. Mariah and I cooked it," she said smiling. "Do you like it, Daddy?"

"Oh, baby, it is the best pie I ever tasted," he said savoring the bite, leaning back and rubbing his stomach.

The child ran to Mariah and hugged her, "Oh, thank you. It made Daddy so happy." Then she began to cry.

"Why are you crying?" asked Mariah, bending down to be eye to eye with the child.

"Come here baby," Cass said swallowing, "Why are you crying?" Jenny ran over to Cass.

"I'm so glad you're happy, Daddy," she hugged him and tried to stop crying. He picked her up and kissed her and sat her on his lap. Then she quit crying and started smiling again. She laid her head on his chest.

Cass shot a confused look at Mariah. She also was confused by the child's behavior.

"I could not have made you happy without Mariah, Daddy," Jenny told her father, placing her little hand on the side of his face. She looked over at Mariah and said in her sweet child's voice, "Thank you, Mariah."

With that Mariah also started to cry and ran upstairs. She sobbed hard and let everything out: her mother's death, the funeral, and the new position she had undertaken.

Later a light tap sounded on the door. Mariah stopped crying long enough to say, "Come in."

Cass was not good at consoling a crying female. He felt like a bear with boxing gloves and his words were awkward, "Look, don't cry. She thinks she said something wrong. Uh, uh—come down and read to her or something, please."

"Yeah, give me a minute. She was just so excited. Sometimes her ways just touch me so," Mariah said through her tears, "Tell her I'm just happy. Between you and me, I should have done this at my mother's funeral. I guess I have held it in too long."

"Yes," Cass said, knowing how he would feel if he lost his mother. "Well, dry your eyes and come on down." He left, shutting the door.

Mariah dried her eyes and went downstairs. She read Jenny a book until it was bedtime. Mariah was extremely exhausted and headed up the stairs to bed after she kissed Jenny good night.

That night Mariah fell into a deep sleep. She dreamed off and on of the Nakano. She saw it clearly. She was laying down in the grass and it came closer and closer. She could feel its breath on her face. These were the same yellow eyes that she had seen in her dreams before. She awoke abruptly and was sweating profusely. She went downstairs for some fresh air. As she walked out onto the front porch, she breathed deeply of the cool night air. She looked out into the night and listened to the rain pouring down.

"What the hell are you doing out here with no clothes on?" Cass said angrily. He had been unable to sleep and came out to the porch to sit. He could not believe his eyes when Mariah came walking out with just her oversized T-shirt on.

"I had a bad dream. Sorry," she meekly said, totally embarrassed. She turned to go back inside when the night filled with the terrorizing scream of the white lion.

"He's really close! Quick, get inside!" commanded Cass.

But Mariah was mesmerized by the sound. She was unable to move. Again, the big cat let out a bone-chilling scream.

"Mariah! Mariah!" yelled Cass, grabbing her arm. "I said get back in the house."

"I dreamed of it. Just like Nooka the old Native American woman told me I would," she whispered to herself. She turned and looked up at Cass with a confused and terrified face.

Wolf started to scratch on the door, barking to get outside. Wolf's barking had brought Mariah back to reality and she acknowledged this was not the place to be. She turned and went in the house.

"Strange," Cass said under his breath as he followed her in. He was becoming a little disturbed with the fast pacing and low growl from Wolf. The dog was clearly alert, stopping every so often, trying to move his ears to capture all sounds. A long, deep growl came from the dog's throat, then a howl. Mariah had gone upstairs to put on her jeans and a T-shirt and came back down after hearing Wolf howl. She herself was unnerved by Wolf's actions. She looked questionably at Cass. He said nothing. Wolf suddenly shot to the back porch, growling louder. Both Cass and Mariah followed him but wouldn't let him out on the screened in porch. Wolf wanted outside badly. He paced and he growled.

Looking out across the backyard Cass and Mariah saw the sky light up with lightning. For a few seconds both stood face-to-face staring at the white cat, which stood only feet away from the house. It had stopped and was looking straight at them. At the same moment the cat gave an ear-piercing scream.

"My God!" Cass said in disbelief. "I'm getting my gun." They both returned to the front room.

"It will be gone in a minute," Mariah said, almost hypnotized.

Ignoring her remarks Cass went to his cabinet and got a gun and loaded it. When he returned, he said, "Go to Jenny's room. If she wakes up with the sound of the gun you will be there," Cass commanded.

"He's gone. Look at Wolf," Mariah said, calmly petting Wolf as he laid his head in her lap.

"I don't care. I'm going to shoot some shots in the air to make sure he is gone and that he does not come back," he explained to her.

Mariah went to Jenny's room, woke her, and prepared her

for the shots. The child jumped then seemed to drift quickly back to sleep. Mariah kissed her and covered her back up.

"Go on back to bed," Cass said as he put the gun away and locked the case. He now came to the scary thought of what might have happened if Mariah had not gone out on the porch. Would the white lion have jumped him? He would have been an easy target just lying there on the bench. He turned to look at her but said nothing.

"It won't be back tonight," Mariah offered as she walked up the stairs.

CHAPTER THIRTEEN

Cass and Mariah awoke early. They both entered the kitchen at the same time but said nothing of the events that went on the night before. The rain had subsided, making the grass greener and the trees glitter. Cass took his coffee and went to the back porch. It was one of his favorite places; he and Jenny's mom would sit for hours at night just talking. He missed it so much. His thoughts turned again to last night. Was he dreaming he saw the cat only a few feet from his house? He went outside to look for proof. Sure enough, Cass found the tracks of the big cat just feet from the house. Now he was sure it happened. He had to go talk with Cub's great-grandmother. He had overheard Ben's story. Seeing the cat this close to his house and the strange way Mariah was acting last night made him curious and nervous. He needed to find out more.

Mariah walked out of the house and saw the tracks Cass was looking at. She knelt and placed her hand in the print. She shuddered.

"I'm going to town. Don't leave the house until I get back," Cass said softly, "I need to find some answers. Mariah, you acted so strange last night. Maybe it would be better if you and Jenny went also."

That was the first time she heard him say her name when he wasn't yelling at her. There is nothing like hearing your name in the morning after a good rain! "I did? Sorry," she said flushing, and then turned her head. She wondered if she should tell him of the meeting with Nooka yesterday but decided against it. "It is so beautiful here," she said, changing the subject.

"Yes, it is," he agreed looking at how the sun highlighted her hair. He quickly looked away.

"What are you guys doing out there!" yelled Jenny from the porch, making both Cass and Mariah jump.

"Just looking around," Cass answered. "Stay in the house baby. We are coming back in."

They ate breakfast and went to town to see Nooka. While they were driving through town, they went past Doc's house. He was just loading his station wagon with supplies. They stopped and talk with him for a while.

"Good morning, where are you off to so early, Doc?" asked Cass.

"I'm going to Nooka's to check her leg. Where are you three going?" Doc said with a big smile. It was nice to see them all together, including Wolf in the back.

"That's where we are going," said Cass, "Come on and squeeze in and go with us."

Doc threw his bag in the back and climbed in. Mariah was forced to move next to Cass and put Jenny on her lap. Cass became very aware there was no way he was going to be able to shift gears without touching Mariah's leg. The first time his hand slipped off the gearshift and grazed her knee, Mariah instantly turned red. Cass was clearly uncomfortable. Doc was enjoying Cass being so uncomfortable.

"Let's stop at Ted's so I can get something to eat," Doc said.

"Geez, Doc," Cass groaned as he turned the truck to go back to the grocery store.

"Stay in the truck. I'll just be a minute," Doc said smiling to himself and thinking he just might take his own sweet time. He was really enjoying this.

Doc jumped out and immediately Mariah moved over away from Cass. It seemed a very long time before Doc came back, stuffing the last of a sweet roll in his mouth.

"Come on, Doc, hurry up," yelled Cass.

"Yeah, OK," he said, wiping his hands before getting into the truck. "That was great!" he said, smiling, when Mariah had to get back over by Cass.

"Glad you enjoyed it," Cass growled.

Mariah was again forced to move over next to Cass. She sat so close she could smell the soap he showered with that morning. She had a good view of his large arm reaching for the gearshift and felt his hand touch her leg each time he shifted gears.

"Why are you going to see Nooka?" Doc asked.

Cass told him the story of what happened the night before, leaving out some of the details because Jenny was in the truck with them.

"Are you sure? You saw him in the backyard?" Doc questioned.

"Yes, when the lightning lit up the sky it was standing no more than six feet away from the back door while we were in the screened-in porch. It was looking right at us," explained Cass. "Listening to old Ben's story I wanted to talk with Nooka, and I want to see the pelt. This cat I saw last night was unbelievable. It was snow white and the biggest one I have ever seen."

Doc pointed up the road at a black van. Cass knew instantly whom it belonged to.

"It's Grey's," Cass said as he pulled up behind the van.

"Stay in the truck until I come and get you," Cass ordered Mariah and Jenny.

Doc and Cass both went into the small cabin. Cub had just showed Grey the white pelt. Grey was trying to buy the pelt from Nooka.

"They said it was not for sale," Cass told Grey.

"I'll give you one thousand dollars for it, Indian. That's more money than you will see for a while," Grey offered again.

"It's not for sale," said Cub. "That's final."

"Fine, you probably bought it anyway and dreamed up the whole story," Grey said and spit on the floor.

Nooka was sitting on the couch with her sore leg propped up. She couldn't see Grey but could feel his bad spirit. "Why don't you go out and find your own pelt?" she asked him. "Just go into the woods with your gun and wait for him. He has not eaten for a couple of days. He would be easy to find."

"I will get your pelt, old woman, after I kill and skin mine. Keep it here for now," Grey threatened and turned on his heel and left.

Cass followed him out the door. "Grey, don't come back to Nooka's."

Grey had not heard a word Cass had said. His attention was on Mariah sitting in the truck. He walked over and smiled his toothless grin.

"Mornin' ladies," he taunted. Wolf growled a warning from the back.

"Hi," Mariah said quietly. Jenny turned and buried her face in Mariah's chest. Cass reached in front of him and opened the door. He grabbed Jenny and held her while he helped Mariah out of the truck.

"Nice family. Yeah, nice family you got there, Cass," Grey said, looking Mariah up and down.

"Don't come around Nooka's anymore," Cass ordered as he walked Mariah and Jenny into the cabin, "Wolf stay!" he directed the large dog to stay and guard the front door.

The large lion wandered most of the night. Something as old as time had pulled it from its sleep last night and unnerved him. He went searching in the pouring rain. Something made him go to the human's house. He had looked into their eyes, satisfying his curiosity. When he left the sound of gunshots sent him running for his life.

But now in the early morning he grew hungry and sniffed long and hard at the sky. The search for food began. His ears perked to sounds in the distance. He stood facing the sound, his eyes glaring, his lips pulled back in a silent snarl. He held his head in the air and sniffed again. The scent of food started his tail twitching. He moved stealthily toward the scent.

On one of the streams shores that fed into the lake, two young Native American boys sat fishing. They had caught only a few fish up shore and decided to move down the shoreline. Both had been warned by their elders not to go too far from the village, but down the shoreline their luck had improved so they moved further and further away from the village. The boys chattering and laughter could be heard by the searching lion.

The white lion crouched in the undergrowth, watching his prey. Instinctively it would try for the smaller of the two boys. The huge feline slowly advanced, keeping in the crouched position. It was like a phantom as it quickly leaped on his target, striking him on the shoulder and breaking his neck instantly. It dragged the kill into the undergrowth and was gone as quickly as it had appeared.

The child that was left on the lakeshore sat paralyzed for a minute, unable to move after the horror he had just witnessed. As soon as he realized what had happened, he started to scream and could not help but wet himself as he started running home. His yells unnerved Wolf, sitting on Nooka's porch. The large dog barked and scratched the door until Cass came out. Cass could see Wolf wanted him to follow him.

"Cub!" yelled Cass, "Something is wrong." Cass could hear the boy's yells and saw him running toward the large group of Native Americans running toward the boy. He could see Grey's van had stopped and was watching the scene unfold. "Mariah, stay here with Jenny. Go Wolf," He said and motioned for Wolf to go ahead.

Cass and Cub went over to the crowd. Wolf was already beside the boy, licking his face. This seemed to calm the boy.

The boy started to tell the crowd what had happened. After the child had told the story he turned to his mother and said, "We were just fishing." More tears streamed down his face. "The white lion jumped on him and took him away into the bushes."

Cass shot a look to Cub. He knew the small brothers were Cub's sister's children.

"Can you show us where the lion attacked?" Cass asked the little boy.

"Yes, can we take Wolf with us?" asked the young boy, holding on to the dog.

"No!" said Grey, forcing his way through the crowd, "I'll get my dogs."

Cass knew Wolf would chase the cat and by instinct try to kill it. Wolf wouldn't have a chance against the big cat.

"Get your dogs; I'll have Doc run and get the sheriff," Cass told him.

"Jamie!" Cub yelled at a young Native American woman, "Go tell Great Grandmother what has happened and hurry."

"There is no hurry," Grey said flatly, which made the young woman stop and turn to look at him, "You know the boy is dead, probably half eaten by now."

The boy's mother, Shana, let out a scream, falling to her knees.

"Grey, do you have no feelings?" Cass angrily asked, although he knew the statement was probably true.

Many women helped the child's mother to her feet. Cub went to her and placed his hand on her tear-stained face and said, "Be strong. Take the child you still have and go. I will bring the other son home."

Cub's sister stopped her crying and shook her head yes.

Jamie took a hold of Cub's arm and asked, "The spirit cat has taken one of us. Will you hunt it now?"

"No," answered Cub. "I go only to get my nephew's remains."

Jamie turned to walk to Nooka's cabin to tell her of her great-great-grandson's fate. Jamie could not figure out why Cub did not hunt the lion, especially now that it had killed one of them.

Cub followed Cass to his truck to get his guns. Cass pulled a rifle from his toolbox in the back of the truck and loaded it. Doc walked outside and was quickly told of the missing child. Cass instructed Doc to take the truck and get the sheriff then went into Nooka's cabin, ready to tell Nooka they were going to go get her great-great-grandson. Cub came in and found Nooka with tears streaming down her face. Cub knelt to his great-grandmother's side. "Great-grandmother," he said and took her hand.

"Go find the remains of my great-great-grandchild," the old woman said.

"Mariah, stay here with her. Keep Jenny and Wolf inside," instructed Cass.

"You are going," she asked.

"Yes," Cass answered, seeing the worry in her eyes. "We are not going to hunt the cat, just to find the boy," he added to reassure her. It was a great feeling to see her worrying about him. This brought a strange feeling to surface.

"Is Grey going with you?" she asked. She could not believe she asked him this. She bit her bottom lip, trying not to plead with him to not go.

"Yes, he is taking his dogs," he replied, and he and Cub went to leave. Cub turned and gave her a weak smile and shut the door behind him as he left.

Mariah was a little concerned about Grey going and Jamie could see this in her face. Jamie quickly patted her on the hand and said, "Don't worry, Cub is going also."

This is what worried Mariah. She remembered Grey saying something about saving a bullet. She knew Grey could in fact accidently shoot Cub. It would be hard to prove otherwise; she was sure Grey could stage it.

CHAPTER FOURTEEN

The young Native American woman named Jamie stayed with Nooka and Mariah. Nooka introduced Jamie as being Cub's intended bride as soon as she turned eighteen in just two months. Mariah was glad to see Cub had someone. The young woman had Native American features, but by her blue eyes and long, light brown hair, Mariah could tell she was only part Native American heritage. She would learn later that Jamie's mother had left and gone to Seattle to find work when she was younger. She came back after two years heavy with child. Most of the tribe shunned her but Nooka told them the child would be a girl and would someday marry her great-grandson Cub. Jamie's mother passed away when Jamie was young. After her death, Jamie was finally accepted by the small tribe. Now Nooka's words, like so many other times, would come true.

"Nooka, I dreamed of the white lion last night," Mariah said in attempt to change the sad mood of the cabin.

"So, did I," admitted Nooka. The white film of the cataracts made her eyes appear gray. "I walked with you in the clearing and lay down in the grass with you. I did not move and awoke when I could feel his hot breath on me."

Mariah was stunned. "Nooka, that is exactly what I dreamed," Mariah told her. She looked over at Jenny and when she was sure Jenny was sleeping, she continued. "I woke up when I felt its breath on me. I was hot and scared. It was so real. After I woke up, I walked outside to cool off and get some fresh air. Cass was up and sitting outside on one of the benches. Before we went back inside, I heard it. It was so close. Its scream was like nothing I have ever heard before. We went inside on the back screened-in porch. Lighting lit up the sky and there it was. For a brief second, I looked into its eyes. My first thought was how beautiful it was. But now this, it has killed a child."

"To the lion the child was food," Nooka told her. "Sounds like you might have saved Cass's life. The dream you had was a warning the white lion was sneaking up on your loved one. The death of my great-grandson should have never happened if I would have thought about my dream and taken the warning. I know the dreams to be real and that we must listen to them. I, at first, did not listen or believe in the dreams until the white lion killed my brother."

"Loved one? Cass is not my loved one," Mariah corrected her.

"Yes, he is, and you his," Nooka countered, "You don't know this yet nor does he. Listen to your dreams Mariah, they are a warning."

The white lion feasted until he was full. It covered its kill and searched for somewhere to sleep. Lazily it padded through the undergrowth until it found a rocky hill, then climbed straight up the rocks. It always searched until it found a ledge that looked over the valley. Finding the perfect spot, the lion began cleaning its thick white coat. In the distance, it could hear hounds. This was of little concern to him and he quickly fell asleep.

Grey had allowed the dogs to sniff the young boy's clothing. Cass, Cub, the sheriff, and Grey took off following the dogs, straining on their leashes. They came to the place on the lakeshore where the boys had been fishing. The dogs sniffed and found an obvious trail through the thick undergrowth. It was slow going in the dense growth.

"Are you prepared for what you are going to find?" asked Grey. "There will not be much left."

Cub and Cass looked at each other but did not say anything. Neither of them had thought about what to expect. The closer they got to the body the louder the dogs bellowed.

"We're getting close," Grey informed them. "You know the lion is probably not far from the kill. Do you want to hunt him?"

Cub looked at Cass and the sheriff then answered Grey, "I am taking my nephew back. I did not come to hunt the spirit cat."

"You are yellow, Indian. What about you, Cass? I can let the dogs loose and they will find the cat and keep it occupied until we get there. Then, we just shoot it," Grey said to Cass, smiling his toothless grin.

"Your dogs don't have a chance if they run up against this cat," Cass said simply.

"They only track the animal. They will not attack it. They have done this before many times. Maybe not with a mountain lion, but I have never lost a dog. These three are my best and if I should lose one or two, I have reserves. At least we will have a chance to kill the beast," Grey said with excitement, "Come on, Cass, don't you want to give it a try?"

"No, not today." Cass answered, and then went on to tell the story of the cat's visit to his house last night.

"You should have called me," the sheriff told him.

"Mariah saved your life," Cub said simply. "The cat would have for sure picked you off that porch. Great-grandmother used to tell of her dreams of the white spirit cat. It was like they were somehow connected. Her dreams could almost predict the next kill."

"Indian, the only connection here is it is a coincidence," Grey told him. "Cass, if that lion was at your back door last night that means it crossed the bridge and walked a hell of a long way to make the kill this morning. I do not believe that. You must have been dreaming. Whoa! There is the boy." Grey stopped his dogs, "Here, Indian, hang on to my dogs."

Cub held the dogs as Grey uncovered what was left of body.

"Not much left. Give me the bag," Grey ordered.

"No, I better do this," the sheriff said and bent down to place the remains in the small body bag.

"Well, if no one else wants to hunt the cat I guess I'll go by myself," Grey said, unleashing his dogs.

The white lion was awakened by the closeness of the bellowing hounds. It jumped to its feet, tail lashing from side to side, eyes fixed on the area of the sound, which was growing closer by the minute. In an instant, it turned and swiftly climbed up the rocks.

The lead dog bellowed loudly after catching sight of the lion scaling the cliffs and let out a loud signal to the others. But the large cat was up the cliff and down the back before Grey reached the dogs.

The white lion crossed the rock-filled shallow pool beneath the small waterfall that fed into the lake. The snow of the mountains had not melted enough yet to make the current dangerous, nor the pool deep. The act of crossing the pool would cause the dogs to lose the scent.

It had taken Grey most of the day to figure out the cat had left the mountain of rocks and crossed the pool. His dogs were not easy to convince that the cat was still not somewhere on the mountain of rock. He had to leash them and pull them away. He went back empty handed. The white lion had outsmarted him and his dogs. This only made Grey more determined to find and hunt the fairy tale.

CHAPTER FIFTEEN

Pastor Bob had heard of the child being killed by the white lion and went to Nooka's cabin.

"Nooka, is there anything I can do?" he asked.

"Pastor Bob," Nooka said, "The Great Spirit has my great-great-grandchild. If our great spirits are the same, then the child is in good hands."

"True, Nooka, but is there anything I can do for you?"

"Yes, ask the Great Spirit to give Mariah strength. She will need it in the next few weeks."

"Mariah, yes, I have heard of you and I am very glad to meet you," Pastor Bob said as he shook Mariah's hand, "Is there a particular reason why she would need extra strength?"

"She will be the one that will rid the valley of the spirit cat," Nooka told him.

Pastor Bob said nothing, only smiled at Mariah. He had learned to respect what Nooka predicted.

"Nooka," Jamie asked, "Why will it be her and not one of the valley's people?" She had been listening to Mariah tell Nooka some of her life story and could not believe the great spirit would find someone from so far away to do this.

"Jamie, we will talk later," Nooka reassured her.

"I will pray for Mariah, Nooka. Where is the dead child's mother? May I go see her?" asked Pastor Bob.

"I will take you," Jamie offered. "Mariah, I will return. Tell Cass thank you for helping Cub. And thank the man that helped with his dogs."

Shortly after Pastor Bob and Jamie left, Jamie came back

and told them the sheriff, Cass, and Cub had returned with the remains of the boy. She also told them Grey had taken off by himself to hunt the cat.

The remains of the boy were taken to Doc's for examination using Cass's truck. It would be the next day before the tribe would get the remains back for any ceremony.

Cub took Cass, Mariah, Jenny, and Wolf to Doc's office to get Cass's truck. They waited for Doc to finish examining the child's body. The sheriff and Cass sat and talked about the white lion while Mariah and Jenny played in the yard.

"I think I will try to get some more help hunting the cat," the sheriff said. "Soon the logging company will be running full-time and lots of people will be at risk. I have contacted my niece who works with animals from New Mexico. She'll be here soon. She has lots of experience with tracking. She has even been to Africa and went out in the bush to hunt down animals that had turned into man-eaters."

"Too many people might not be a good idea. But with Grey in the valley I think your niece might be in danger. Grey cannot be trusted with women." Cass went on to tell the sheriff how he could not stop looking at Mariah and how Grey had only this morning been at Nooka's trying to purchase her pelt.

"You don't have to worry about my niece. She is one woman I would hate to make mad. Grey is an odd character, isn't he? What would you like for me to do with him, Cass? I can run him out of the valley if you like," offered the sheriff.

"No, he really hasn't done anything yet. Let's try again with what we have. Grey is out there right now trying to get the cat. Let's not get too much more help yet. Maybe we need to set a trap. Mariah, take Jenny and Wolf home in the truck. I'll have the sheriff bring me home," Cass ordered. "Don't leave the house. Sheriff let's go make a plan and get the men we need. When Grey makes it back, we will ask him to help."

Mariah drove home and found Cass's brother Matt and his

wife Connie pulling in the driveway when she got there. Matt looked a lot like Cass but smaller.

"You have got to be Mariah," he said, smiling.

"Yes, Cass is in town with the sheriff. They are planning to hunt the white lion. It killed one of the Native American children today," Mariah told him.

"Yes, I heard that Nooka's great-great-grandchild was killed by the lion. We will go see if he needs any help. You and Jenny stay inside."

"Yes, it was nice to meet you both," Mariah said, and waved goodbye to them.

Cass and the sheriff sat at McCain's waiting for Grey to return. They had planned to tie up a lamb and wait for the cat. It was nearly dark when Grey walked into McCain's. Grey reluctantly told them of the smart tactic the cat pulled on his dogs.

"Why don't I just camp out by your place, Cass? Seems like that cat likes to visit you!" Grey mused as he poured down his fourth shot of whiskey. He caught the look Cass gave him and said no more.

A very tall, large-framed woman entered the Tap and ran directly into Lewis James, who was attempting to walk out the door. "Whoops," she said as the man fell into her. She stood well over six foot and was strongly built. She easily held the man up. "Where ya going, buddy?" she asked.

"I, I, I have to go take my daughters home. They are in the car," he slurred. She, like most everyone in the bar, had asked him if they could take him home but he had refused. He became angry and irritated with her and waved his arms until she let him go. He looked up at her and saw her size. "Sorry, lady," he stumbled, caught himself, and continued to stagger out the door.

The woman watched the man leave and shook her head. She looked around the bar and saw the sheriff. "Uncle Pat is that you?" the woman asked, walking to the sheriff.

"Beth, Aunt Pearl's Beth?" the sheriff questioned, a little

shocked by the size of her. She was as tall as him and probably weighed close to his weight and she looked more like her dad than her mom. But her smile was addictive.

She smiled because she understood he not seen her since she was small. "Yes, I hear you have a white mountain lion in these parts. I would like to hunt it and maybe capture it for a zoo," she said, taking a chair, turning it around, and sitting on it backward.

"Why?" Grey demanded. He had seen the woman come into the bar and like most of the others in the bar could not stop staring at her. She was not a bad-looking woman, but he thought she awfully masculine.

Beth looked at the new toothless man. She gave the man a death gaze and said, "Because it is rare. People would come and see it," she said, her voice stern. "So, I guess you could say for the money. I will split the money with anyone that helps me," she yelled to the patrons of the Tap. Two men raised their hands. They had asked Grey to hire them to help hunt the cat and he had told them he worked alone with his dogs.

"I don't care who gets it, how they get it, or when they get it, just as long as they get it before the church social," the sheriff said. "I can't imagine what would happen with all those people out in the open with that lion on the loose."

"I will do my best, Uncle Pat. I will be staying with you until I set up a camp. I am excited and have full confidence that I can capture the lion," she said and was about to go on when Grey walked over to the table and spit chew at her feet.

"That lion is mine, dyke!" Grey cautioned. "I intend on killing it, skinning it, and keeping the pelt."

The sheriff went to stand to stop Grey from bad mouthing Beth, but Beth was not intimated by Grey. She out weighted him by close to seventy-five pounds. She stood up towering over him six inches. She looked down showing him he did not intimidate her. "Yours? Ha! We will see who the better man is," she said quietly and smiled.

"You're on, dyke!" Grey left to prepare for the next morning. He would let his dogs loose and they would track the cat. All he would have to do is find them. This she-bitch would still be in bed when he shot the lion.

Beth shouted out to the patrons of McCain's, "I have two men but need one more. I will pay one thousand a piece the first week." Quickly she had her three men and they sat down as she instructed them on a plan for the morning.

"Well, seems we don't have to run our plan now, Cass. Surely between Grey and Beth they will get the cat. Let me take you home," offered the sheriff.

Cass's brother Matt came in before they got out the door. Cass thanked the sheriff and hitched a ride home with Matt and Connie. They stayed at Cass's house for a couple of hours talking. Mariah found out they had three boys age seven to ten and that Grandma and Grandpa were keeping them so their parents could get out of the house. After they left Mariah put Jenny to bed and found herself on the screened in porch thinking about the day.

"You shouldn't be sitting out here," Cass said, coming out into the screened-in porch. She said nothing but came into the back porch that had the security of all the glass in the windows. This was a better view anyway, she thought to herself. She sat there watching the sun go down. She must have fallen asleep in the chair but was awakened by Cass's cursing.

"Damn," she heard him say. She walked into the kitchen. Water was leaking everywhere. Cass was throwing everything out from under the sink. She rushed to get some towels to sop up the streaming leak.

"Open that cupboard and get my toolbox! Get me a couple of wrenches out of it," he was surprised when Mariah handed him the tools so quickly.

"It is leaking in two places. Get under here and hold this for me," he ordered from under the sink.

Mariah crawled into the other side of the sink. She grabbed the wrench, her face only inches from his.

"Lie down on your side so you have some leverage and hold the wrench here," he instructed.

She moved to her side. Cass's wrench slipped and they both were sprayed with water. Cass again placed the wrench and tightened it. She held the other wrench, trying to tighten and stop the spray of water. They were both drenched.

"I'll hold them. Reach behind my head and turn off the water. Do you see where the turnoff is?

"Yes," Mariah said, blinking the water out of her eyes. In order to get to the turn-off valve, she would have to crawl on top of him, on the side he was in, and reach over his head.

"Hurry up, these wrenches are heavy," he said softly but firmly.

Mariah crawled on top of him, trying not to touch him but there was no way she could avoid it. She tried holding herself up. It wasn't working because she needed both hands to move and find the turn off valve. She slowly laid her body over his and reached around his head. His beard tickled one side of her face, so she moved, her breath catching in her throat.

"Find it?" he asked in her ear. He could feel her breasts on his chest. The wetness of their clothes and the thin cloth of her shirt let him feel everything. His breathing quickened. He was angry he could not control his body.

Finally, she found the valve and asked, "Which way?"

"Right," he instructed.

"Got it," she said and quickly lifted herself off him.

He said, "Get in the other side in case I need you," he said irritated, not wanting her to see the swelling in his jeans. He tried to think of something else, but it was useless. This angered him further and one of the wrenches slipped and struck Mariah on the shoulder hard.

"Oh God! I'm sorry," he said. "Where did it get you?" he asked, picking her up by the waist and scooting them both out from under the sink. When she could she rolled off him on her back holding her shoulder.

She was trying not to cry and was slowly attempting to get up. She was taking deep breaths and said, "I'm OK," she lied. "It's like hitting yourself on the funny bone. I'll be OK." She really thought something might be broken until she was finally able to move it.

"Need some help getting up?" he asked. He was feeling bad, which helped take the swelling in his pants down.

"No, give me a minute."

But looking at her lying prone on her back wasn't helping the situation. He could see her nipples through the front of her wet shirt. He quickly grabbed a dry towel, holding it in front of him on the pretense of drying his hands.

"Are you sure you are OK?" he asked impatiently. He sounded angry and grew angrier at the loss of control of his body, and the fact that it wasn't going away.

Mariah took a deep breath and painfully got up.

"Yes, I'm fine," she said wondering why he was mad at her when he was the one who hit her with the wrench.

"Look, I'm sorry," he said. When she stood her breasts heaved against her wet clothing. He wanted to reach out and touch one and his breathing quickened. "Go in the other room and I will finish this," he said, turning and facing the counter.

"I need some ice to put on my shoulder. Could I use that towel?" she asked.

He handed her the towel and remained turned toward the counter.

Mariah pulled her T-shirt down and saw her shoulder was turning purple and starting to swell. She determined it was not broken because she could still move it.

"Let me see it," Cass said. He took a hold of her sleeve and rolled it up. "Oh, that looks like it hurts. Better get out of those wet clothes," he said turning around quickly, fighting the urge to touch her. He went to the sink and fiddled with the faucet.

Mariah wondered why he seemed so detached and uncaring. She put the ice in the towel and went to the dining room. As she sat there, she wondered if he had done this on purpose. No, he did seem like he was sorry. The ice felt good on her shoulder but soon her teeth were chattering from the cold and her wet clothes.

Cass was mad at himself. His life was so much more uncomplicated before her. He struggled to get the vision of her in her wet shirt out of his mind. He finished fixing the leak and the more he thought about her, the madder he got at himself. He was putting the things back in the cupboard when Mariah came back into the kitchen.

"How's the shoulder?" he asked, trying not to look at her.

"It's OK. I can do that," she said.

"It is done. I'm going to bed," he said and quickly left the room. He had to leave. One look at her shirt and he could not trust himself.

Mariah could not figure out why he didn't like her. She was aroused when she touched him. Her face turned red when she thought about it. She had never been that close to a man and she smiled and remembered the feeling. It felt good but why did he have to be so mean? She placed the ice in the sink and went to bed. Her shoulder ached and she found it difficult to sleep. She didn't dream of the white lion, but of Cass.

Cass lay in his bed going over every detail of the evening under the sink over and over. He could feel her breasts on his chest, smell her, and see her face next to his. In the middle of the night he got up and took a cold shower so he could get some sleep.

CHAPTER SIXTEEN

"Mariah," Jenny said softly, "It's morning; time to get up."

"Oh, what a sweet little alarm clock you are," Mariah said, hugging her. Pain shot through her shoulder, "Ouch!" she said and pulled up her sleeve to see the ugly purple bruise.

"What happened?" Jenny asked.

"Just a little accident," Mariah said, getting up. She dressed then helped Jenny.

"Where is your dad?"

"He went outside. Said he would be back before breakfast," Jenny answered, watching Mariah fix her hair, "Can you do that with my hair?"

"Sure," Mariah put Jenny's hair in a high ponytail and curled the end. Her shoulder was painful, so she took some aspirin.

Mariah was cooking breakfast when Doc came walking in. "I brought some rolls!" he said, grinning. "Where is Cass?"

"Outside somewhere," Mariah answered.

Doc walked out the back and yelled. Cass came from the forest area with Wolf by his side.

"Mornin'," Doc yelled. "Are you going to Nooka's great-great-grandchild's ceremony?"

"Like to," Cass answered, clearly thinking of something.

"It's this evening at eight. Do I hear dogs?" Doc asked, turning his head toward the sound.

"Yeah, Grey is camped less than a mile from here," Cass said, going into the house. "He is convinced the lion will be back here."

"I hear the sheriff's niece is going to try to capture it," Doc said as they entered the kitchen.

"Yeah, you ought to see her. She is over six feet, must weigh well over two hundred pounds and has arms as big as mine. She and Grey have a bet on who will end up with the lion," Cass said, smiling.

"Really, the sheriff said she was a little strange. She worked for the zoo for years and has even been to Africa. He didn't seem to be too worried about her going off into the woods with three men," Doc joked back as he walked back into the house.

"Doc! Doc!" yelled Jenny, "You must fix Mariah's arm. She had an accident."

"Accident?" Doc asked, giving Mariah a shocked look.

"I hit her with a wrench," Cass admitted.

"You hit her?" Doc asked, turning toward him with a shocked look, "Good Lord, man, why did you do that?"

"No. No," Mariah giggled, "it was an accident."

Cass looked relieved, "We were under the sink fixing a leak."

"Oh, well let's take a look," Doc said, pulling the neck of her shirt down, and then raising her arm. He gave Cass a questioning looks over his glasses and shook his head in disbelief. "Did you put ice on it?"

"Yes, as soon as it happened," Mariah answered.

"Well I think it will be OK but if the pain and soreness doesn't subside in forty-eight hours let me know and I will give you some pain medicine." Again, he gave Cass a questioning look and Cass ignored him and sat down at the table. They all ate breakfast and Cass agreed they would pick up Doc before they went to the ceremony.

Cass told Mariah about Grey camping only a short distance away. He was going to his parents' and brothers' homes and didn't want to leave them alone, so they went with him for the day. First, they stopped at each of Cass's brothers and warned them about Grey camping so close. Mariah was glad to finally meet all his brothers, their wives, and children. They were all going to the ceremony that evening.

They ended up at Cass's dad's house. He was getting ready for the logging company and sawmill to open.

"It's been a long winter. As soon as the snow melts, we can start moving some of this lumber," Henry told his son, smiling. Cass was a spitting image of his father. This warmed his father's heart when people told him this. He wished Cass was happy. He stood there listening as Cass brought him up to date on Grey and told him about the sheriff's niece and her pursuit of the lion.

"Are you going to the ceremony tonight?" he asked his father.

Cass's father gave his son a sad look and said, "Nooka needs our support. Your mother and I will be there. She has been a good friend to the family. I hate to think of giving Grey five thousand dollars, but if he gets rid of the lion it would be worth it. I can't very well see the sheriff's niece wanting to keep it alive but guess as long as they get it out of the valley I don't care."

"Grey said the lion crossed the pool under the waterfall. That means it is on this side of the valley again. Be careful, Dad," Cass said, "I would feel better if you carried a gun around for a while."

"Good idea," Henry said, looking out across the valley.

The white lion again looked for food. It didn't try to return to its kill from yesterday after the hounds followed him. He had left the valley floor and the next day had traveled halfway up the mountain. He smelled spoor of a female and followed her scent far up the mountain. Soon he recognized the call of the female and found her lying on the ground, rubbing and rolling in the dirt. He became very excited and instinctively started toward her, wailing. He began to whistle back to her, his lips slightly puckered, his whiskers arching forward. The adult female mountain lion hurried toward him. The two met in the small clearing. The white lion, brash and very anxious, advanced toward his intended mate. To his surprise and alarm the female raised her front paw and smacked him. He jumped back and shook his head. He advanced again; his body crouched low in submission. He whistled and cooed, pleading to the wary female. He quickly moved sideways as her paw again struck at him. Now from a distance he stopped and studied her. She became coy and started to purr, stretching out lavishly. He continued to stay back and watch her. This move is what she wanted and came to him and started licking his face. He in turn started licking hers.

CHAPTER SEVENTEEN

Doc, Cass, Mariah, and Jenny, along with Wolf, parked the truck and walked past the many cars parked for the ceremony. The Native Americans were dressed in ceremonial clothing. Nooka and her family sat watching a native dance and ancient burial ceremony. After this, Pastor Bob said his Christian words over the small casket, per Nooka's request. The casket was lifted by members of the family. They led the procession of lanterns and torches to the burial grounds. The Native Americans sung a low, sad-sounding song.

When they reached the burial ground, they gathered around the small grave that had already been dug and slowly lowered the casket. The child's mother threw a handful of dirt on the casket. She shed no tears because she knew her son was with the Great Spirit and walked with his ancestors now. Nooka was led to the grave and threw a handful of dirt, followed by the rest of the tribe.

Everyone was invited back to the ceremonial circle to help the child's spirit rise to the sky to meet the Great Spirit. Food had been prepared to share with the spirit before it left. Then everyone feasted and danced into the night.

Mariah sat holding Jenny as they watched the Native Americans dance. Cass's brothers, their wives, and children sat by her, enjoying the food and dance. Cass sat talking to his mom, dad, and Doc. When Cub could he came and sat by them.

"Thanks for coming," Cub said. "Looks like most of the town is here."

"McCain's will probably go broke!" Edna Hart commented. They all laughed.

"I hear that the sheriff's niece is trying to capture the spirit cat," Cub commented, "I think that is a big mistake. Someone is bound to get hurt."

Nooka yelled for Cub. He went quickly to her side.

"Help me over to the Harts and then home, please," she asked him and took his arm.

"Nooka, you are in our prayers," Edna said to her, reaching up and taking Nooka's hand.

"Thank you, Edna. I need to tell you all that Mariah holds the outcome of the white lion," Nooka slowly told them. She was visibly tired, and it took a lot of effort to stand.

Cass turned to look at Nooka then looked at his parents. All were quiet. Cass looked down at the ground.

"Henry, your father has told you the last story of when the Nakano came the last time and what role I played. The Great Spirit now has picked Mariah for this role. She is the one. She does not totally believe this yet, but her dreams will guide her. I pray for her because I know the strength she will need. Take care, my friends, and keep those close to you from harm's way. The spirit cat can't be captured, nor can it be killed by a man." Nooka turned away from them and Cub walked her back to her cabin.

Mariah sat far enough away she did not hear the conversation. She looked up to see the Harts, Doc, and Cass all looking at her. No, they were staring at her. She felt very uneasy and looked away.

Jamie tapped her on the shoulder, and said, "Mariah, please come and walk with me." Judy reached over and took Jenny. Mariah and Jamie walked some time without speaking.

"Nooka has talked with me. She asked me to help you in any way you need," Jamie stated. "I really don't understand why you were picked. I was hoping it would be me."

"Jamie, I'm not so sure I know why this is all happening, nor if I totally believe this. I am not so sure I am ready for it. I am totally confused and don't know how I became involved," Mariah confided in her, "It's a far cry from Kansas and the small-town life I came from."

"I myself have never left the valley," Jamie said, "I live to marry Cub. I do not understand why the Great Spirit went to Kansas to get you when I am here, but I must accept what is destiny, and Nooka's request that I help you in any way I can. First, I will tell you when you dream you should tell the dream to Nooka, no matter what. Do not leave the valley until your mission to rid the spirit cat is finished. And finally, you have to go through a ritual with Nooka."

"What ritual?" Mariah stopped walking and asked.

"Some ritual you and Nooka will do," Jamie told her, shrugging her shoulders.

"And when will I do this?" questioned Mariah.

"I'm not sure what day but Nooka said sometime in the future. She will let you know," Jamie explained, "Just remember to tell Nooka of all your dreams of the spirit cat. Now we better turn back. They will wonder what we are doing. Does Cass know?"

"I think so, but I don't think he believes it. I am not sure I believe it. But I know he thinks I was acting weird the other night when the lion was at the house and wonders why I acted so strange."

"Strange?"

"Yes, it was like it had me under a spell."

Jamie explained, "You are both putting each other under a spell. You are drawn to each other. Someday you will understand this."

Jamie's comments were disturbing to Mariah. How could she put that large animal under a spell? They walked back to the gathering in silence.

Cass found her and angrily asked, "Where have you been?"

But before she could answer he said, "Come on, Doc, she's back; we can go now." He angrily motioned her to the truck.

After saying their goodbyes to friends and family they drove home in silence. Mariah went to bed wondering what Jamie meant by helping her but quickly drifted off to a deep dream sleep.

She was walking up the mountain and climbed up on a high ledge. She turned and saw the white lion after her. There was no way the cat could reach her way up here. But as she blinked the white cat grew to twice its size and easily jumped up on her ledge.

Mariah awoke soaking wet with perspiration. She got up and walked downstairs. She went outside and stood on the porch, breathing in the cool, night air. Feeling refreshed she heard the far-off bugle sound of the dogs. They must be on the trail of the white lion. Maybe Grey would get it tonight and she would no longer be haunted by it in her dreams.

"Are you OK?" she heard Cass say from inside the screen.

"Yes, just had a bad dream," she answered, feeling a little embarrassed again only clad in her oversized T-shirt. He must have been standing there watching her for a while.

"Want to talk about it?" he asked from still inside the house.

"No, what time is it?"

"Midnight," answered Cass

"I'm going back to bed," she said and opened the door. She walked past him, avoiding his eyes. She didn't look up as she walked the open stairway and felt him staring at her. He must think I am crazy, she thought to herself.

Cass had been sitting in the front room. He had heard her call out from her sleep and was ready to go up and see if she was OK. Then he saw her come down the stairs and directly go outside. He had observed her trying to catch her breath and how frightened she looked. He recalled Nooka's words of how Mariah's dreams would guide her. He took a deep breath, not knowing what to believe, and went to bed remembering how distressed she looked. He wanted to comfort her, and he again was mad at himself for even thinking about such things. After all, she was just a nanny to his daughter. That's it. He would not allow it to be any more. It hurt too badly.

CHAPTER EIGHTEEN

Mariah was up early and had started breakfast. She woke Jenny up before Cass came downstairs. When Cass walked in the kitchen Mariah was teaching Jenny how to stir up biscuits. Unaware of him staring at them he watched how patient Mariah was with Jenny. He smiled to himself as he watched them. Jenny poured the ingredients in after Mariah had measured. Both laughed when Mariah set the flour sack down on the counter a little too hard and a cloud of flour came up, falling all over the counter. "What's going on here?" asked Cass, making them both jump up.

"Daddy!" Jenny yelled. "We're making biscuits."

"How long have you guys been up?" Cass asked.

"Long time," Jenny said, "We went for a walk then we—"

"A walk?" he said angrily, "You went outside?" He could not believe Mariah took his daughter outside. He flew mad and walked outside to cool off. When he returned, he sat down at the table.

"We took Wolf with us," Mariah told him. She could see the anger cross his face and braced herself for his next words.

"Wish you would not do that until I get up," he said sternly.

"Sorry," Mariah said, thinking his response was mild compared to what it could have been. "Doc is coming over for breakfast."

"Did he call?" Cass asked, thinking he couldn't believe he would sleep through the phone ringing.

"No, I called him," Mariah answered, not wanting him to know that she had called Doc to tell Cub she needed to talk to

Nooka. She wasn't sure how she was going to be able to tell Nooka about the dream. Nooka didn't have a phone. Mariah wouldn't be able to get to her house without Cass asking questions. So, she had called Doc and told him she needed to talk to Cub.

"Why did you call Doc?"

"Just had a question about my shoulder," she lied, feeling bad about lying to him.

"Is it worse?"

"No, just a little sorer than I think it should be. I just need something to help me sleep," she lied again. Her mother had once said that one lie would soon lead to more.

"Oh," Cass said and walked outside with Wolf, feeling guilty about her shoulder. He couldn't hear Grey and his dogs anymore and wondered if he had moved camp. He would go find out before breakfast. When he got close enough, he could see the camp was abandoned and Grey had moved on. He was so relieved he whistled as he walked back to the house. His whistle was cut short when he heard Jenny yelling. Cass started running toward the house. Wolf bounded past him. As he got to the driveway, he saw Cub punching Grey in the jaw and throwing him into his pickup.

"Don't come back!" Cub said slamming the door.

Jenny ran out of the house and flew into Cass's arms. "Daddy, he was hurting Mariah," she sobbed and buried her face in Cass's shoulder.

"It's OK now, baby. Everything is going to be OK," Cass said, trying to calm her. He was furious and yelled at Grey, "I better never catch you around my home again or I swear I will kill you." Doc came outside and took Jenny out of Cass's arms and took her back inside. Cass thought about what would have happened if Cub had not been there. He was enraged at the fact that Grey had little thought about Jenny seeing what had enfolded. He started toward Grey's truck with the full intention of pulling him out of truck and beating him within an inch of his life. But Grey quickly started the truck and backed out of the drive before Cass could reach him.

"Don't come back you son of a bitch!" Cass yelled than swung around and looked at his friend Cub. In all his days of growing up with Cub he had never known him to fight or hit a man. Cass could see his jaw was bruised and his lips were swollen and bleeding. His eyes were dark embers of fire. Cass was glad he was on his side. "Are you OK?" he asked.

"That man is bad," Cub said trying to find control. "Where were you?" he asked with a puzzled look on his face.

"I took a walk to see if Grey was gone from the campsite. Jenny said he hurt Mariah," Cass said, trying to change the subject. He was feeling guilty for his walk.

"I don't think she is hurt, but he really scared her. Doc and I had just got here and saw Grey's truck. I could not believe you had let him in the house and then I heard Jenny screaming that Grey had ripped Mariah's shirt off. He said it was an accident," Cub said with a phony laugh. "Let's go see if she's OK. Jenny was upset; she saw everything."

The thought of Jenny seeing what Grey did to Mariah enraged Cass. Grey had ruined a beautiful morning in just a few minutes. He remembered his daughter's fear and ran into the house. He remembered her wide, fearful eyes and grew angrier. He found her in Mariah's arms on the couch. They were hugging each other with Doc by their side.

"Daddy, that man hurt Mariah!" she cried and ran to him. Her big tears streamed down her face.

"It's OK," he said, patting her on the back and hugging her close. He looked at Mariah. She had changed her shirt and looked OK other than being upset; he could tell she had been crying. "Are you all right?" he asked her, trying to decide if he should ask just what Grey had said or done and decided not to. He had a pretty good idea.

"Yes, I thought it was you coming back inside. I didn't even

◆ 104 ◆

turn around. If Cub hadn't come in when he had—" she said but could not finish before she started to cry again.

"We could call the sheriff and have him placed in jail," Doc recommended.

"No!' said Cub, "I think he will think twice about coming here again. Between Cass and me I think he will be very discouraged about ever coming back."

"When I see him, I will take care of the rest of it," Cass said quietly and looked at his friend Cub, and they both nodded.

"When I leave here, I will go and find out where he has moved his camp," offered Cub. Cass was sure within a couple of hours Cub could find the dogs and Grey.

Doc stood and exclaimed, "Mariah and Jenny had made a beautiful breakfast of biscuits and gravy. We need to all sit down and eat something."

Cub left and nodded again to Cass. They all sat down to eat breakfast and soon were all laughing again.

"Mariah did Doc look at your shoulder?" asked Cass as she was clearing the table.

"No, not yet," she answered not sure how she was going to tell Cub about her dream. Now what was she going to do?

"What's the matter?" Doc asked.

"My shoulder hurts and I am just not able to sleep very well," Mariah said as she carried the dishes over to the counter. She heard Cass say something but couldn't hear what he said. When she returned to the table Doc said, "Mariah, I can give you something to help you sleep but I would like to look at that shoulder. Let's go into the other room."

They went into Jenny's bedroom and Mariah told Doc she needed to talk to Cub to relay a message to Nooka.

"Just tell me and I will tell her. I have to go check on her leg today," Doc said

"No, you wouldn't understand."

"Try me. Nooka told Cass and me the story. I am aware of Nooka's prediction," Doc told her, "She tells us you will be the one that will take the spirit cat away. Just tell me what you would like to tell her."

Mariah was a little taken back. She wondered why Cass hadn't said something.

"She wants me to tell her my dreams of the white lion," Mariah said, and told Doc all about the dream. Doc gave her some medication to help her sleep and looked at her shoulder.

"Boy, you really do have a large bruise there. Just how did this happen?" he asked with a serious look. "Did you just stand there while he hit you?

Mariah giggled and told him the real story of how she was hurt.

Doc laughed and said, "I wish Cass wasn't so ugly sometimes. Course his heart was broken when Becky died, and he just can't seem to get over it. Hang in there, honey."

"I will, Doc. Thank you for relaying my dream to Nooka. Oh, listen, we have company," Mariah said after hearing laughing and another female's voice.

"It's Gus and Judy," Doc said as they left the bedroom and walked to the kitchen.

"Hi, Mariah," Judy said, "All of us girls are going to the city the end of the week to buy a dress for the church social. Would you like to go?"

"No, but thank you," Mariah answered remembering Jamie's warning about not leaving the valley.

Cass was about to say that Mariah couldn't go because she had to watch Jenny, but Mariah's answer caught him off guard.

"Well, can I get you a dress? You are about a size eight, right?" Judy asked.

Cass was about to answer the question again when Mariah said, "No thanks, I have a dress."

"So, you are going to the church social with Cass and Jenny?" Judy asked ignoring her brother-in-law's dirty look.

"I don't know about that, but I want to go to church and

Cass told me I could," Mariah answered Judy, not looking at Cass.

Gus was sitting at the table enjoying the discomfort he saw in his brother's face. He could remember his brother's words about Mariah not going to the social. He knew exactly what his wife was up to and was glad he had told her of Cass's conversation.

"Of course, she is going; I'm picking them up," said Doc also enjoying Cass's uncomfortable look and Judy's pressuring. "Isn't that right, Cass?" Doc winked at Judy.

"Never thought about it," answered Cass. He turned and looked out the window. He continued to look out the window and ground his teeth.

"I'll pick you up about eleven a.m. OK?" Doc asked.

"Yeah, yeah, fine," Cass said, not wanting to further the conversation.

"We came out to tell you that Grey moved his camp to the area where Uncle Jeb was killed," said Gus, changing the subject.

Cass explained to them what had just happened this morning. Gus was on his feet, clearly angry by what had happened.

"Mariah, did he hurt you?" asked Judy.

"No, I'm fine. He just grabbed my shirt and it ripped it off when I lost my balance and fell. Thank God Doc and Cub came in right then," Mariah answered with a shudder.

"Did you call the sheriff?" questioned Gus.

"I'll take care of it," Cass told him. Now he knew what happened to her without asking. He was shocked by the anger he felt about Grey touching her.

"I'm sure you will," Judy said, smiling at her brother in law. She knew Cass was not one to get on the bad side of. Grey was in for a surprise.

CHAPTER NINETEEN

The sheriff's cousin Beth had tracked the white lion up on the mountainside. She was surprised to see that he had left the valley floor. Maybe this was a good sign. They had made camp on the mountainside and Beth had decided to stay the night. She and her men rose early to go look for further evidence of the cat. She had sent her men in the opposite direction this morning. They were a little concerned and questioned her on why she was going out alone. She just smiled at them and told them to meet back at the camp in two hours.

She now was on a steep upward climb up the mountain. After a period, tired, hot, and thirsty, she sat down on a rock. She had found the first tracks at the break of dawn and it had been uphill ever since then. She took a few sips of water from her canteen and gazed downward. Looking down toward the valley she saw a maze of trees and beyond them, Elk Lake. It was beautiful. This was a place she could live, she thought, and remembered how her Uncle Pat had taken her and her brother camping. Her brother wasn't much for camping, but she loved it.

She had climbed high enough that the trees were less dense and large rock ledges were scattered between them. She looked to the left and the right, seeing lots of ground cover, but the trees now were spotted on the hill.

Beth started to climb again and slipped on a small rock. Looking down she saw the large tracks of a cat and a scat mound. It was fresh, damn fresh. Her heart pounded. She must be very close to the white lion.

The white lion was the one who found Beth. He had been aware of her presence and the others long ago. The white lion had been resting on a ledge when the woman's scent reached him. He had killed a goat the night before just outside of a house. It had been a small goat and he had carried it up the mountain to a safe place, and the woman was getting close to the partially covered remains. The lion wasn't hungry, and this creature's smell was a little different. Curious, he set out to find who was intruding on its domain. Beth's scent to the cat was like a fingerprint. He could identify her from all other humans and could detect no danger in her scent.

Beth sat down on a rock and was sure the lion was close. The only gun she had was a dart gun and she loaded it and sat it on her lap.

The white lion had watched her sit and load the dart gun. He remained still as he observed her. Despite the whiteness of his coat he blended in well to his surroundings. Beth began talking out loud, "Come here, kitty; it is better if I get you instead of Mr. Grey."

The lion's ears twitched. He was intrigued.

"Here kitty, kitty," Beth continued then laughed nervously.

The laughter startled the cat and he jumped. The movement caught Beth's eye. She saw the white lion for only a moment and met the unblinking yellow eyes staring back at her. Then it was gone.

"God, you're beautiful," she said aloud, thinking of the magnificent animal she had seen. After she saw the snow-white shining coat of the cat, she knew Grey would stop at nothing to get it.

It was noon so she headed back to camp for lunch. She hurried down the mountainside, anxious to tell her men what she had just seen. Twenty feet from camp she stopped when she heard Grey's voice. She had to bury her excitement as she entered the camp.

"Grey, you must not be having any luck either," she said and threw her pack down.

"You expect to find the cat just walking around?" Grey laughed. "Want to borrow a couple of my dogs?"

Beth had to hold in her glee. "No thanks. The cat must be on your side of the valley. Do you mind if I move my camp closer to yours?" Beth said, trying to convince him the white lion was not close.

"Sure, come on over; we'll share a sleeping bag." Grey said and smiled a toothless grin.

"No, thanks, you're not my type," Beth told him boldly looking into his eyes.

"What is your type? You want a soft female, probably shorter than you, dyke?" he asked again with a toothless grin.

Beth offered no comment to the obstinate man. She just smiled and planned on keeping him guessing.

"Did you ever meet the woman that is taking care of Cass Hart's daughter? She's a beauty. I copped a feel this morning; could have gotten further if that damn Indian hadn't shown up," Grey said, shifting his crotch area, trying to impress the men in Beth's camp.

"Cub? I remember him when I was a kid visiting here. He is not a man to mess with Grey, nor is Cass," Beth warned him, disgusted with his story.

"Cub is not a man; he is just a damn Indian!" then Grey went on to tell Beth about the white pelt Cub's great-grandmother had and her claims of how she got it.

"Yeah, Uncle Pat was telling me something about it. He told me she still has the pelt," she said, standing very straight to show Grey he didn't intimidate her.

"Yeah, I saw it. It made me want the white lion more than anything. I am telling you this for your own good: I will stop at nothing to get it, so beware," Grey said moving closer and standing with his mouth open. He reached up and massaged one of Beth's breasts.

She grabbed his hand and twisted it back, creating obvious pain for him, and said, "Well, like I said, let the best man win. Do you want a bite to eat before we break camp?" she said to him, still holding his arm in a twisted position, which she knew was hurting him badly.

"No, I'm going back and try to find some tracks then turn my dogs loose. Thanks anyway. That offer about sharing a sleeping bag still stands. I guarantee you'd be a satisfied woman."

"I will keep that in mind," she said as she let her hold go from him.

He stumbled back and caught himself. He stood there looking her up and down, rubbing his wrist. He turned to leave, and taking one last look, winked at her before he left.

When Beth was sure that Grey was gone, she told her men of her encounter with the white lion and that she was going back up the mountain tomorrow first thing by herself to see if she could find the lion again. One of the men told her he thought Grey would stay around here and wanted to know if she needed some protection. She thanked the man and told him she could take care of herself. She had seen many of Grey's kind before. She laughed at herself, remembering him thinking she was a dyke. Sadly, she thought of her friend Brian in Africa. He was English and a little on the heavy side and much shorter than her, but they had fallen in love with each other. He was a veterinarian working for the government who had been hired to vaccinate a tribe's cattle. She planned on getting this white lion and selling it to a zoo so she could go back to Africa and be with him. He had asked her to marry him, but she had wanted to come back to the U.S. and tie up some lose ends before she committed. She had been away from him for two months and she missed him very much.

She was very aware of her size and stature. She had always been the tallest in school and in college most of the boys thought she was gay because of her love for the outdoors; she never had any boyfriends. She never did until she met Brian. She fell asleep thinking of him.

The next morning early Beth took a two-way radio with her and instructed her men to wait for her to call. She had planned on darting the animal the moment she saw it, then call her men to bring up the cage and get down the mountain before Grey had any idea what was going on.

Beth climbed back to the place where she had seen the cat. She searched the area and found a mound that was certain to be the white lion's last kill. She backtracked to where the lion had stood staring at her. She found fresh tracks and began to follow them. She climbed a high rock ledge and looked around. As she looked to the left and higher there the cat stood staring back at her. She could see all of him. His yellow eyes were staring, not blinking at her. His mouth was slightly open, revealing his great ivory fangs.

Beth was transfixed. She stood still, staring at the yellow eyes. She feared that if she made a movement for the dart gun he would be gone. Then he slanted his yellow eyes and opened his mouth and made a low sound. He was warning her to stay away. He knew she had found his kill but when she did not touch it, he followed her out of curiosity.

Beth sensed the danger and slowly backed down off the rock. When she looked back at the ledge the lion had closed its mouth and seemed to stare at her through softened eyes. On impulse she began to talk to the animal in a calm voice.

"You are so beautiful. If I don't ever do anything ever again, I have been granted one of life's greatest pleasures," she said to him. Was he purring? She thought she could hear the cat start to purr. He yawned and sat on his haunches. The purr became louder and Beth was overjoyed.

Abruptly the lion quickly stood and stopped purring. He was looking down at the valley floor, studying something far away. He turned his head toward Beth as if to say goodbye. Suddenly, with incredible speed, he sprang away. Beth blinked her eyes then climbed back on the rock, "What happened?" she asked aloud. Then she heard the distant sound of the dogs, "Grey, you bastard!" she said climbing in the direction the white lion had gone.

The barking of the dogs was very close now. Beth tried to cross the tracks of the lion, but the rocks made it unclear which way he had gone. She was beside herself, but there was nothing she could do so she just sat down on a rock to wait. The dogs had found the cat's last kill and now bugled when they found the fresh trail. Three dogs were now visible to Beth and she watched them climb the rocks. They ran past her and continued to follow the scent. In a few minutes she heard the scream of the cat.

"Damn!" she said. Bewildered she almost got up and left but then she heard the yelp of one of the dogs, another scream from the cat, another yelp, and another. She waited. Next, she heard the cat let out a shriek of pure rage, which filled the wilderness. All went quiet, an unnatural absence of sound.

The dogs had obviously gotten too close to the cat. The white lion had quickly torn open the first two dogs with its claws and they lay fatally bleeding. The third dog was caught by the throat and died instantly. The cat tore open its belly, making sure the animal was dead. He could still smell Beth and knew she was close. He was confused and sensed further danger, but not from Beth. He sprinted off at lightning speed.

Beth was sure the lion had escaped. She couldn't hear the dogs anymore and did not need to go find them to know they were dead. She continued to sit on the rock and wait until Grey came. While she waited, she remembered her encounter with the most beautiful thing she had ever seen. This moment was ruined by Grey. He huffed and puffed his way toward her, climbing up a little at a time.

"Did my dogs come through here?" Grey asked as he approached her.

"Yep, they are further up," Beth answered.

"Don't hear them. That's not a good sign," Grey said walking past her, "Better go bury them. First dogs I ever lost."

Beth smiled to herself and went back to camp.

CHAPTER TWENTY

The rest of the day Cass had stuck around the house. He told Mariah every time he went to go outside and made her lock the door behind him. He worked outside for a while and finally decided to go in for lunch and play with Jenny for a while.

Late afternoon the phone rang, and it was Doc wanting Cass and Mariah to come to Nooka's. She had wanted to visit with Mariah about her dream last night. Doc talked with Cass about how Nooka also had dreams and wanted to compare both their dreams to the future.

The drive to Nooka's found Cass saying very little and Mariah not sure how he felt about all that was happening with her dreams and the white lion. She worried he would think this was all her fault. He had been so angry when Grey had been in the house and she knew his biggest fear was the safety of his daughter.

She stared out the window wondering how she ever became involved with this. She had been dreaming of the white lion's yellow eyes since she was a little girl. Now she knew what the dreams meant. She had never shared them with her mother because her mother was always so busy working and she had no close friends in the little Kansas town. They managed on her and her mother's salary working at a local hospital until her mother became too ill. Mariah thought again of her father. Where was he? His name was Joseph Glory she knew, and her mother shared very little about him, which made Mariah even more curious. Mariah had tried to find just one person who might have known him but never did. Her mom had moved to her parents' house in Kansas, leaving any record of him or where he might be. With no family and no record of friends Mariah had no one to ask about her father. There was just no way to find out where he was, and she now accepted it. She loved Cass's big family and almost felt cheated she didn't have anyone.

When they got to Nooka's Jenny had begged to play with a little Native American girl May who lived the next house over from Nooka. It was agreed that she could only if the little Native American girl stayed and played with her on Nooka's front porch.

Before they went in the house the sheriff drove up. He got out of his car and tipped his hat to Mariah. "Cass, I heard you had a little bit of trouble this morning," he said.

"Yeah, how did you find out already?" Cass asked.

"Small town. I just saw Jim Green, one of the men Beth has helping her hunt the white lion. He was picking up more supplies and told me old Grey was in their camp late this morning bragging about it," the sheriff informed him.

Mariah looked away and her face turned red. She shuddered at the thought of Grey's intentions.

"Sorry, ma'am," the sheriff apologized. "Cass, I'll go run him in if you like."

"No, I plan to handle it," Cass told the sheriff. If he ever got ahold of Grey, he would be sorry he ever came to the valley.

"All right be careful," the sheriff warned. "Oh, one more thing, Beth called me on the radio a little bit ago. Said she saw the white lion, said she got about twenty feet from it and the damn thing just sat there and looked at her and started purring. Can you believe that? Then, I guess somehow Grey had found out she had seen it and let his dogs loose. That lion ended up killing all three of his dogs! It seems like Beth was having more luck than that old skunk. She said she could have almost caught the damn thing if Grey hadn't showed up. She said she got caught up in the moment and didn't dart it like she had planned."

"The white lion is a man-killer; why would she want to get that close to it?" Cass asked.

"Don't know. Beth is kind of a strange one. She has always gotten along with animals much better than humans," the sheriff explained.

"She is going to get herself killed. Can't you talk to her?" Cass asked.

"Nah, she's strong willed, always has been. She was in Africa helping a tribe and a vet down there with a cattle herd. She'd sleep in a tent with no fear of an animal coming through the tent after her," the sheriff said, shaking his head. "She and Grey have a bet going on who can bag that white lion first," the sheriff explained and again tipped his hat to Mariah. "Well if you don't need me, I better get back to work. Don't hesitate to give me a call if you ever want to haul that asshole in. Sorry, ma'am," the sheriff said, again tipping his hat one last time to Mariah and getting back in his car. He had to duck to miss the roof of the truck but smoothly bent his large frame into the driver's side.

Cass and Mariah waved goodbye to him and went into Nooka's cabin to find Doc and Jamie already there.

"Welcome," Nooka said. "Come on in." She smiled bright. Her gray hair was pulled back, making her cataracts even more prominent. "What you dreamed last night tells me now there will be two lions to tend with."

"Two!" Cass exclaimed. "Are you sure, Nooka?"

"Yes, another has come from the mountains and has passed into the white lion's territory. He is not a spirit cat but just as deadly. Please, if you dream tonight please get a hold of me in some way. My dream last night was much like yours. Your dream confirms that there is another lion for sure."

"Nooka," Cass said, "Will this cat also kill one of us?"

"I don't think so. The dream only tells us there are two.

What is important is tonight's dream," Nooka said shutting her eyes. Mariah could tell that Nooka was weary from this ordeal.

"Nooka, I must tell you of the incident that happened with the woman hunter Beth," Mariah said. "She got about twenty feet away from the cat today and the cat didn't attack her. Why do you think this is?"

"I have seen this woman in my dreams. At first, I questioned her place in all of this. I believe she is the one that will help you. She should not ever trust the lion. Mariah, if you see her, please let her know this."

"One more thing, Nooka," Cass said. "Grey let his dogs loose today. The cat attacked these dogs and killed them. Isn't this strange for a lion to do?"

"I would not trust the lion, nor would I expect him to act like another mountain lion. He kills to feed the spirit," Nooka told them.

"I wish this was under control before the church social," Cass told Nooka.

"Yes, that would be a good thing. We all plan to be there. I would like to see the girl who got attacked by the spirit cat," Nooka said.

Doc reached down and patted Nooka's hand. "I imagine she will want to get out of the house. Today I looked in on her and she is bored, and I think also wanting to see her beau," he said laughing.

Nooka now was very visibly tired. Doc had finished wrapping her leg and they all said goodbye and left for home. Cass never said a word to Mariah until they got out of the truck. "I will put Jenny to bed. Go ahead and go to bed if you want," he said as he walked toward Jenny's bedroom.

Mariah went to bed early that night and fell into a deep sleep and soon she began to dream.

She was walking in the forest and came to a clearing with a small brook running through it, and all around her the forest was lush and green. She looked up and saw two small fawns meekly walking out of the forest into a clearing by a beautiful running stream. On the right side of the fawns came a large buck deer; it stood by them. The buck was sniffing the air through large nostrils and Mariah could see the steam of his breath. It was a very peaceful and beautiful scene.

The large buck deer became very still and focused on an area to the left of Mariah. He became very nervous and attempted to coax the small deer into the safety of the forest. In a flash the large buck took off across the clearing, using itself as a decoy and jumped over the creek, coming right toward Mariah. It was within that moment the white lion ambushed the buck, bringing him down to ground. Mariah could hear bones crunching and the loss of air from the buck's lungs when it hit the ground. Now Mariah stood only a few feet away from the scene and could see the white lion tear open the belly of the buck and start eating. She looked toward the little fawns and could see them peeping out from the forest. They stood in shock watching the scene play out before them. When she looked back at white lion it seemed closer. His yellow eyes bore through her as the cat let out an eerie scream that tore at her ears.

Mariah awoke with a scream. She was hyperventilating and perspiration was pouring off her. She jumped out of bed, disoriented and confused. When she realized where she was, she ran out of her room and down the stairs. She was having problems breathing, gasping for air. She unlocked the front door and ran outside, taking deep breaths, gulping the air.

Wolf had awoken Cass with a nudge. Cass, half awake, had heard Mariah's scream. He was sitting in the front room and had watched Mariah run outside. He got up and walked outside on to the porch to stand by her.

"Mariah," he said, "are you OK?"

She turned and looked at him and fainted in his arms.

"Mariah," he said, as he laid her down on one of the

benches. As he held her, he noticed she was drenched with perspiration. Cass watched her as her breaths became shallower and fewer. Her eyes started to flutter and open.

"Mariah, you fainted," Cass said as he knelt beside her. He said it tenderly, which surprised him, making him fall back. He stood up quickly, still looking at her. The porch had a large log railing around it and he quickly went over to lean on it.

"I did?" she asked in a light voice, now becoming more familiar to where she was. She sat up on the edge of the bench and Cass came and sat beside her. She glanced over and saw he had only his jeans on and no shirt. She had never seen a man's chest before up close and something stirred deep inside her. Mariah wanted to reach out and touch the hair on his chest. But the mood was abruptly broken by the scream of the white lion. It had sounded extremely close, and they both stood up.

"Let's go into the house," Cass advised as he walked over to the door and stood. "It's too close."

"Wait," Mariah said listening again for the sound.

"That's not a good idea," Cass suggested.

As he turned to walk across the porch to Mariah, he saw the white lion standing now near the bottom of the steps. Mesmerized, both the cat and Mariah seemed to be unable to move. Finally, Mariah spoke.

"Cass, go into the house," Mariah commanded, "He will not hurt me."

The cat moved closer to the step, ready to walk up onto the porch. Wolf was barking and pouncing at the door. Cass had to do something to keep him from tearing the screen door off. The barking did not seem to affect the cat. Both he and Mariah stood their ground, staring at each other.

"Mariah," Cass said as he opened the door and held Wolf back with all his might, "Step back toward the door."

She took a few steps backward and Cass grabbed her, pulling her into the house and slamming the door shut quickly.

Wolf continued to bark and claw at the closed door. The lion let out another bone-chilling scream and Cass knew it was on the porch. Looking outside he could see the large cat walking back and forth. Cass took Wolf and locked him in the bathroom, and Wolf began to howl and bark.

Cass ran to his gun cabinet and loaded a gun. He was quite shaken, Mariah thought, as she watched him load the bullets into the gun. Wolf became quiet and Mariah softly said, "Cass, he is gone now."

Cass stopped loading the gun and looked at her, "Mariah, I need to do this," he said to her and finished loading the pistol. "Please go to Jenny's room in case the sound of the gun wakes her up." He walked outside to the back porch and shot the gun until it was out of bullets.

The white lion ran through the forest. It had again been called from its sleep by an unknown force. He had been pulled to the human's house and saw into the eyes of something that made him curious but cautious. It fled the porch and the area sprinting when it heard the gunshots. It continued to roam through the night. He was not looking for food. Hunger was not the reason for its travel through the valley. As it roamed it detected another of its kind. It stood sniffing the air; it was another male.

CHAPTER TWENTY-ONE

Mariah had comforted Jenny and waited for her to go to sleep. She brushed hair away from Jenny's face and waited just a little while more and went back to her room. Mariah fell asleep with no further dreaming through the night. She awoke early and sat on the edge of her bed thinking about the dream and not quite understanding her bravery the night before as she stood staring into the eyes of the white lion. She couldn't believe she had done that and stood up, shaking her head in disbelief. She dressed and went downstairs and started breakfast.

Cass awoke earlier and had gone outside to walk around. He had to prove to himself that the cat was here last night. He easily found the cat's tracks and shuddered at the thought of Mariah just standing there staring at it. He didn't understand why she had no fear. God, she could have been killed. A small fear hit his heart. What was she thinking? It angered him knowing this cat was so close to his house and Jenny. He walked up on the porch and sat there.

Cass heard Mariah calling Doc. He heard her tell him of the dream so he could let Nooka know. Cass knew this dream would mean something and probably meant someone else would be killed. He hoped it would be Grey.

Cass stood on the front porch trying to relive last night when his brother Gus drove up in the driveway.

"Isn't it a little early for you to be walking around, bro," Gus said with a smile as he got out of his truck.

Cass gave him a somber look and said, "The white lion was

standing about right here last night," Cass said and stopped at the place on the porch where he had seen the cat. "Mariah was here, I was here, and the cat was here." He stopped talking and looked again at his brother Gus. "What is the matter?" Cass asked him, seeing the confused look on his face.

Gus was now shaking his head back and forth. "It killed Mike Potter's prized stallion last night," he told Cass.

"Not the black stallion?"

"Yep, right next to the barn, about eleven last night," Gus stated to him. "What time was it here?"

"That's when it was here," Cass said, remembering Nooka's reading of Mariah's dream. "Proves there now are two of them. Do you know where Grey is?" Cass asked again.

"Two of them?" Gus asked.

"Yes, Nooka said now there are two. Do you know where Grey is?" asked Cass again.

"He was the first one on the scene," Gus told him, shaking his head. "Yep, not sure how Grey finds out things so quickly."

"And Beth?" Cass asked.

"Don't know where she is, no one has seen her," Gus said, observing Cass staring off in deep thought.

"Look the reason I came over is that all the wives went shopping and won't be back until dark. Do you want to go over and start on some of those logs? Mom went too, so Dad is out there by himself," Gus told him.

"After what happened yesterday, I really want to take Jenny and Mariah with me until Grey is out of the valley," Cass said.

"Sure, sure, I understand. I'm going over now. Just in case, I have a handgun with me," Gus told him, patting his side where he carried the gun.

After they ate breakfast, Cass loaded Wolf, Jenny, and Mariah in the truck and took out for his father's house. It would be good to do some physical labor and get his mind off the cat and his growing feelings for Mariah.

The white lion had not rested since he had detected the intruder in his domain. Midafternoon the cat came upon fresh spoor. He could tell the spoor was the male intruder. The big cat's mission now was to run this intruder out of his territory. If the other cat chose to fight, the white lion would fight to the death to keep his region.

A familiar scent came to the large cat's nose while he journeyed. Beth and her men were traveling across the edge of the valley. They were looking for fresh tracks and were not able to find any. They had heard that Mike Potter's stallions had been killed last night from the sheriff. Beth could not believe that the white lion had backtracked, but the dead stallion had confirmed it. She could not believe the distance between the areas. It didn't make sense to her. The cat would have to run in order to get across the valley that fast.

But it had not been the white lion. The intruder had killed the stallion. It now lay on a rock ledge above Beth and her men watching the caravan make its slow progress.

"Let's stop and rest." Beth said putting her pack down. "We'll go ahead and set up camp here. I am going to go scout out above us."

Beth took off up the mountain. Despite her size she ambled easily up the mountain. She was in great shape. Most men would be breathless.

She looked for any signs of the white lion. When she came upon a fresh scat pile and fresh tracks she was overjoyed. She assumed it was from the white lion. But it was from the intruder. She began to climb again.

Suddenly the white lion was curious about Beth but caught the scent of the other male lion. He spied the intruder cat readying itself on the ledge to jump on Beth. A low growl came from the white lion's throat. His curiosity of Beth was soon forgotten. He moved up the mountain quickly toward the intruder's scent.

The intruder was a very large two-year old male in great shape. This intruder was aware another mountain lion in the area, but the young lion was ready to do battle for territory of its own. Now the intruder was fully stalking Beth and had not detected his rival being so close.

The intruder waited on a ledge for Beth to get closer. At the precise moment the young cat leapt at Beth, the white lion leapt at the young cat. Both cats landed only feet from Beth, locked in a fearful embrace. Beth fell backward, frozen with fear.

They fought furiously and the wilderness echoed with their screaming and snarling. Beth backed up and watched in amazement and couldn't believe that she had a ringside seat. She began to relax and tried to stand but her legs were like JELL-O. She knew she should probably take shelter and get the heck out of there, but she could not tear herself away.

The contest of domination of the valley took about ten minutes for the white lion to win the battle with his well-armed adversary. Beth was shocked to see the lions fight until death. This was unusual. Most of the time one lion would break away and find another domain.

When the white lion was sure the intruder was dead, he took several swipes with his large claws to the motionless body, snarling loudly. Beth was still standing close to where she had fallen backward on her backside. The white lion's yellow eyes locked with Beth's. For a moment she held her breath because she was not sure what the cat would do. Again, she had only her dart gun. The cat was the first to break the stare down and turned, racing down into the valley.

Beth sat for a long time not moving but thinking until one of her men yelled at her. "Beth! Are you all right?" yelled the man, racing toward her. "Did you kill this lion? Thought he was white?"

"It was amazing," Beth whispered. She cleared her throat and said, "They fought to the death, right here, right in front of me." She got up and looked at the dead mountain lion. It then occurred to her that this dead lion would have killed her if it was not for the white lion. "It saved my life," she said to her man. "If it had not jumped this lion, I would be dead." Beth decided right then and there she had to save the white lion. A new respect for it flooded her. "He saved my life—very unusual, very weird," Beth said still a little shaken.

Beth and her men carried the dead mountain lion into town. They told the tale of how the white lion had ambushed this cat while it had stalked Beth. It was a great story. The reporters from the valley were hanging on every word and writing everything down.

"That is unbelievable, Beth. Good job but don't take chances like this. You need to make sure one of your men is with you from now on," said the sheriff.

Grey had been sitting at the bar listening. He was getting angry and had heard just about enough of this story. Over and over they had told the story to every person that came into McCain's. Soon, Grey had heard enough, and his anger wouldn't allow him to listen any longer. He got up from his chair and turned to leave. He bumped into Lewis James, a frequent visitor of McCain's. Lewis staggered to keep standing. He fell and attempted to stand but the blow of Grey's body had knocked the wind out of him. He finally just sat on his backside looking up at Grey.

"God damn drunk. Go home!" yelled Grey at him, cursing again as he walked out the door.

Beth helped Lewis James up off the floor and said, "Hey, mister do you need a ride home?"

"No, I got it thanks," Lewis said to her and staggered out the door. Lewis stood still for a moment and tried to remember where he had parked his car. Through hazed eyes he had spotted it and with much effort he staggered to it and opened the door.

"Daddy's home," Lewis said as he stuck his head in the car. "Are my little darlings sleeping?"

A very sleepy, "Yes Daddy" came from five- and six-year old Sally and Sarah in the back seat. They had grown accustomed to falling asleep in the car when their dad got himself detained at McCain's. Since their mother's death a short two months ago, their father found it hard to go home. He would not allow anyone to keep the two little girls, so they went everywhere with him.

Lewis started the car and sat there for a few minutes before he decided to take off. He drove off, swerving continuously, and fought going to sleep. About five miles out of town Lewis did fall asleep. The car ran off the road down a steep ditch and stopped. Lewis still had his foot on the gas pedal, but the car was hung up and would not move.

Sarah and Sally screamed the entire time until the car stopped. This had awaked Lewis. He looked around trying to figure out where he was. It slowly came to him that he was in the car but stumped at why the car had stopped. He then realized that he had run off the road and the car was not moving. He shut the engine off, left the headlights on, and opened the car door. Lewis fell out of the car and angrily stood and staggered, shutting the door hard. He walked around the car to assess the damage. When he got to the front of car, he could see what he was hung up on. He stood facing the car and laying both hands on the hood of the car was preparing to push the car off the place it was hung up on. He looked through the windshield and could see his small daughters, their eyes as wide as saucers.

That was the last thing Lewis saw before the large white cat pounced on him. He died quickly.

The two little girls saw the white flash but wasn't sure what it was. They just knew that their father was not standing any longer and something white and furry stood over him. Both cowered between the seats, cradling each other.

The Hart women, tired of their long day of shopping, were now back in the valley only miles away from home. They had filled the trunk with packages. It was a good thing they had left the city when they did because there was not an inch of space left in the large trunk. They were all tired and quiet as they turned off the highway onto the gravel that took them home.

Judy was driving and Edna Hart sat in the front. All were happy about their great purchases. Shopping in the big city is something they didn't get to do often, because it took all day to drive, shop, and drive home. Connie, Sue, and Joan sat in the back seat with their heads on each other's shoulders almost asleep.

"Are those lights in the ditch?" asked Edna as she strained her eyes up ahead.

"Yes, I believe it is!" Judy answered. "Looks like someone ran off the road into the ditch. Do you have a flashlight, Edna?" The women in the back seat were now wide awake and straining their eyes, attempting to make out what was in the ditch.

"Yes, in the glove compartment," Edna answered.

Edna opened the glove compartment as Judy maneuvered the car off the side of the road, behind the car in the ditch. Edna turned on the flashlight and pointed it toward the car in the ditch. There was a flash of white. This alarmed the women. All of them screamed and locked their doors. Joan yelled, "What is that? I think that was the white lion standing over someone!"

"Yes, get the heck out of here! Hurry get to Cass's house!" yelled Edna, her voice next to hysterical.

The woman sped off to get help. They said very little until they turned into Cass's driveway. Judy stopped the car abruptly and they all tumbled out of the car, shutting the doors quickly and running to the house.

Cass had heard the car come into the driveway far too quickly and the abrupt stop. The last time this happened he remembered it was Johnny bringing Carrie to them. His heart went into his throat. He went to the door to find out what the problem was. "What is wrong?" he asked seeing the fear in the women's faces, now looking to make sure they were all there.

"Quick!" said Judy, visibly shaken and running all her sentences together. "Call the sheriff and Doc! Someone ran off the road a few miles up and when we stopped to see if there was anyone in the car, we saw the white lion standing over a body!"

Mariah thought of her dream. There had to be children involved. She hurried the women to the table and told them she would make some tea and hot cocoa. She motioned Cass aside and told him to go look for children in the car.

Cass called the sheriff and Doc and told them he would meet them at the site. Mariah made small talk to calm the frightened women. She could see Edna was very shaken, and it took a time for the levelheaded woman to gain her composure. Mariah called their husbands and had all of them come over. None of the women wanted to drive themselves.

"It was a good thing no one got out of the car," stated Connie. "I was just about ready to grab the flashlight and go see if anyone was hurt." They all looked at each other, knowing that this would have been a deadly error.

When Cass was sure the women would be OK, he left and went to the accident. The sheriff and Doc had just pulled up also.

"Have you got a gun?" yelled Cass to the sheriff. "I just don't want that lion sneaking up on us."

"Yeah, I have one. Looks like Lewis James's car." The sheriff said. "Do you think the little ones are in there?"

"I don't see Lewis in here," said Cass looking inside the car.

"Yes, the girls are in the back. God, they look scared to death." Cass opened the door and lifted the little girls out. "I will put them in my truck," he said to the sheriff, who was standing in front of the car looking down.

"OK, Cass, then come back down here. I think I found Lewis," the sheriff said in a tone that Cass knew meant he better hurry.

Beth and her men pulled up when Cass was putting the children in his truck. The sheriff had called her on the radio to let her know that the women had sighted the white lion at the accident.

"Hi Cass, what's going on?" asked Beth.

Cass made sure that the truck door was shut, and they were far enough away so the children could not hear. "I think that Lewis didn't make it. Let's go down and see what the sheriff found," he told her.

"This is all that is left of him," said Doc. "Suppose the children saw the lion kill their dad? It's a wonder they didn't get out of the car."

"Oh my God, I'll take my men and see if we can pick up a trail," Beth said

"Want to do an autopsy?" the sheriff asked Doc.

"Yes. Bag what we have, and I will do what I can and call the funeral home. What on earth are we going to do with these children? Now that Lewis is gone, there is no other family left," Doc told them.

"I will take them for the night," Cass said. "Sheriff, let me know what you find out about them tomorrow." Cass thought to himself that he was truly thankful that Mariah was there tonight. Then it struck him. The dream Mariah had dreamed had unfolded right here. The hair on the back of his neck stood up.

"Doc, Mariah's dream, doesn't this sound just like it in a way?" Cass asked.

Doc looked at him and blinked. "Damn, real close isn't it. I am going to have to tell Nooka first thing in the morning."

The sheriff and Doc went back to town and Cass returned home with the two little girls. He could tell by all the vehicles that the men were waiting to see what had happened. Cass came in carrying the little girls and told Mariah to help him put them to bed. Cass realized that neither of them had uttered a word since they were found. They lay in the big bed hugging each other, their eyes closed. Mariah and Cass looked at each other, both feeling pity for the little ones.

When Cass and Mariah came downstairs, Cass told the story of what they had found. Mariah gasped and whispered, "My dream—it is just like my dream."

"What will happen to those little girls?" Judy asked.

"Probably go to a home. They have no family left," explained Cass.

"Honey?" she said looking at Gus. They had tried so many times for a girl. Gus felt like he had failed Judy by not giving her a girl. This would be perfect.

"We will talk about it later," Gus said, winking at her. He had no problem taking on these little girls after four boys. They had built a huge home with lots of bedrooms. There would be no question in his mind. But he would need to make sure this was possible before he allowed his wife to get excited about it.

When they all were ready to leave Cass and Mariah walked them out to their cars. Cass carried a pistol just in case. When they had all left, Cass remained outside, sitting on the porch. He looked down at the pistol, thinking he had been taking it almost everywhere. He thought of the church social that was coming up and how things needed to be under control before there were so many people out in the open. He sighed and his thoughts turned to his daughter and how he must protect her. Then his thoughts drifted to Mariah and how incredible she made him feel just being around. He smiled to himself and went into the house. He thanked God for her tonight.

"I'm going to bed," he said to her as he watched her wiping off the kitchen table and picking up dishes. He forced his eyes away from her bending over the table, but too late. Feelings stirred deep inside him and this again angered him. He told himself he must control his body.

"OK, good night," she said, smiling at him, and continued to wipe the counter. Did he just look at her in a caring way? she asked herself. She felt a small flutter in her chest.

He turned and went up to his bedroom and quickly fell asleep. He couldn't control himself from dreaming of Mariah and awoke many times frustrated. He would turn and punch and hit his pillow.

Mariah went to bed shortly after Cass and did not dream this night of the white lion. She had a restful night and awoke the next morning to Jenny's little hand shaking her awake.

"Mariah, who are the little girls that are here?" she asked in her tiny little voice. "Can I give them some cereal?"

"I will get up and fix you all something. Is your daddy up yet?

"Yes, he went outside," Jenny said as she followed Mariah out the door and down to the kitchen.

The little girls were sitting at the table and turned to look at her. The younger girl looked at Mariah and said, "I am Sally; this is my sister Sarah. What is your name? Are you Jenny's mom?"

"My name is Mariah and I am Jenny's nanny," Mariah said to her. "Would you like some cereal or maybe some rolls?"

"Oh, yes please! Can you make some for my sister also?" Sally asked. The older sister said nothing. She continued to watch Mariah make their breakfast. "Jenny, where is your mom?"

"She went to heaven when I was born. She watches over me all the time," answered Jenny.

The little girl carried on a conversation. Mariah grew concerned the older sister Sarah had not uttered a word or attempted to eat anything. Mariah thought she would see if she could get her to say something. "Sarah, I need to know your favorite color?" The little girl stared at her for a while and turned her head to look out the window.

Sally piped up and said, "She likes pink."

Mariah smiled and told Sally she needed to have Sarah answer her questions. Sally got off her chair and stood in front of Mariah and said, "She can't talk right now. Her voice went away last night."

"What happened to make her voice go away?" Mariah asked.

The small child came closer and whispered. "She saw a ghost kill Daddy last night."

Mariah was not sure what to say back to her but thought not to pursue any further questions. Sarah sat quietly looking out the window. She still had not touched her cereal. Mariah thought she would leave the room and see if the sister and Jenny could get her to talk or eat. She went outside and found Cass.

"The oldest little girl isn't speaking or eating. I think she has been traumatized and is just not ready to talk. The littlest answers her questions and told me their father got killed by a ghost last night. I guess being the lion is white it would seem to be ghostlike. I left hoping the little one and Jenny would at least get her to eat something. I think we need to call Doc and let him know about her," Mariah said, looking up at Cass.

"Yes, I know that must have been one of the scariest things a little girl could ever see," Cass said, shaking his head. "I am just not sure what is going to happen to them, but I hope they find a home. I know Judy really wants them."

"Really? That would make her, and Gus have a total of six children! Wow!" stated Mariah, smiling.

Cass smiled himself, looking at Mariah. Gosh she was beautiful. He wondered if she ever had fallen love, ever had a man or had a boyfriend, even did anything other than take care of her mother. He turned away and told himself to think about something else.

Only miles away the large cat settled down under a ledge. He had prowled most of the night after his kill and ran away after he saw the light of the flashlight. He cleaned himself and fell asleep.

CHAPTER TWENTY-TWO

Mariah and Cass went back into the house and called the sheriff.

"What do you think the chances are for Gus and Judy adopting those two little girls? Can you ask Judge Barks what it would take and give me a call when you're done?" Cass asked him on the phone. "Come out to the house and we can talk about it."

When the sheriff got to the house, they went in the other room to talk.

"How are they doing?" the sheriff asked Cass.

"Mariah said not very well this morning. It will take time. Do we know when the funeral will be?" Cass asked.

The sheriff let out a huge breath of air and said, "No. Not sure who is working on it. I guess I need to talk to the funeral home. I don't think Lewis had any plans nor did he have any money to bury himself. The city will have to pick up the tab. Are you OK with Gus and Judy taking the girls? I talked to William Barks the lawyer and judge in town and he said he will draw up the paperwork for them to be the legal guardians or to adopt, whatever they decide."

"Yes sure. One of the girls has not spoken since the ordeal. I think she is shell-shocked. Mariah has been working at getting her to eat something, but nothing has worked yet. She is hoping the other two girls will help to get her to talk," Cass told the sheriff.

"Yeah, bad deal. Do you want to take the girls over to Gus and Judy's or would you like me to take them? Or you can keep them for a while. It is up to you," the sheriff said, leaving Cass some time to think about it.

"I think we should take them over to Gus and Judy's. Maybe all the kids will get the one child to talk. Mariah and I will take them over." The last words stuck in Cass's throat. Mariah and I. Frustrated by how this sounded to him he quickly said, "I will run them over there this morning."

The sheriff smiled to himself but didn't let on he could hear in Cass's voice how uncomfortable it was to say Mariah and I. "OK and I will swing by the funeral home and ask about when a funeral for Lewis can be set up."

After the sheriff left Cass walked into the front room where all three little girls sat on the floor playing with Jenny's dolls. The oldest little girl didn't role-play but only sat holding onto her doll, looking down. Cass felt badly for the little one, but his train of thought was disturbed by someone pounding on the door. He quickly walked over and opened it to see Doc.

"Mornin' Cass and Mariah, how are the girls this morning?" he said as he sat down on the couch watching the girls play.

"Doc, this is Sally and Sarah," Cass said. "Girls, why don't you tell Doc good morning."

Sally quickly stood up and went over and said good morning to Doc. Sarah sat there and stared at her doll.

Doc looked up to Cass and raised his eyebrows. Sally quickly answered for her sister. "She isn't talking right now Doc, but she says hi too."

"Well that is OK. You girls have a good time playing with your dolls and I will go talk to Cass for a while," Doc said as he got up. "Walk with me, Cass," he said as he opened the door to go out on the porch. Cass followed him out.

"Wow. I think I have seen this before. She will come out of it someday. What, are we going to do with the two?" Doc said rubbing his hand over his bald head.

"Gus and Judy are going to try to adopt them. Judge Barks

is drawing up the papers. I am going to take the girls over to Gus and Judy's in a little bit," Cass said, careful not to say "Mariah and I" again.

"Are you going to take Mariah and Jenny with you?" asked Doc.

"Yes, probably I wouldn't be comfortable leaving them here at this point," Cass said, trying to sound nonchalant. Cass looked up when he saw Cub's truck coming into his driveway. "Hey!" Cass yelled teasingly at Cub. "What are you doing out and about?"

Cub gave him a sober look and said, "It seems no one has seen Liz since yesterday and she hasn't showed up for work. I thought I would drive out here and see if maybe you had seen her?" Cub looked away as he asked.

"Well I haven't seen her. She probably went with Grey somewhere and he just hasn't brought her back to town," Cass answered back.

Cub could tell Cass was a little put out with Grey still but went ahead and asked, "Can I use your phone to call the sheriff and let him know she isn't here? Kip McCain wanted me to ask you before I said something to the sheriff."

"Yeah, go ahead." Cass looked at Doc with concern. "Do you think Grey has anything to do with Liz not being in town? I have never known Liz not to show up at work."

"I would not put anything past that man," Doc said as he exchanged the same concerned look. They both waited for Cub to come back on the porch.

"Sheriff is going to get ahold of Beth, his niece, to see if she can find Grey's camp and see if Liz is there. If not, I would have no idea where the woman would be," Cub said as he sat down on the bench beside Cass.

"In all the years I have known Liz she would always take the guys up to her apartment above McCain's. She was a pretty smart cookie. Why would she go out to Grey's camp?" Cass said as Cub sat down.

"Yeah, I know. That is why Kip is so uptight. He said her bed had not been slept in and her purse was still in her room and the door was unlocked," Cub said. "Well, I am going back to town to see if I can help the sheriff track her whereabouts."

"Cub let me know if you find her or not. It is strange. Not like Liz at all not to be at work. Something is wrong," Cass said as he walked Cub to the truck. "You know and I know she would never go out to Grey's camp."

"I will let you know what I find out," Cub said driving out of the driveway and back to town.

Cass watched him drive off and wondered what could have happened to Liz. As he walked back up on the porch, he looked at Doc and said, "This doesn't have a good feel."

"You are right. Liz would never go out to his camp. If she is not back by nightfall, we can bet she might not be back at all," Doc said looking up at Cass. "I am going back to town to find out what is going on. I will call you later."

Cass walked back into the house and told Mariah to load up the girls and he would take them over to Gus and Judy's. All piled into the truck with Wolf in the back. As they drove Mariah couldn't help but see something was weighing hard on Cass. She asked, "Is everything all right?"

"Yeah," is all Cass could come back with. He didn't look at her, hoping she couldn't tell how worried he was. It was noon and if Liz didn't make it to work at ten, she had run into something bad. He thought of Grey and what he was capable of and he tightened his grip on the steering wheel. Damn that man has been nothing but trouble since he got here. If he had anything to do with this, Cass made a mind pack with himself, right then and there. He would tie a rope and a rock around Grey's neck and throw him in the lake.

Mariah watched as Cass gripped the wheel. She watched as his knuckles turned white. Something was wrong. Cub had called the sheriff at the house and said something about how she wasn't there. Who were they talking about? Mariah shuttered as she thought of one of Cass's sisters-in-law getting hurt, or worse yet getting hurt by the white lion. She knew all of them would throw themselves in front of that lion to save any of their children. Fear set in and she froze; tears started running down her face.

"Mariah, are you all right?" Jenny asked as she took a hold of Mariah's face to turn it to hers. "Why are you crying?"

"Just thinking about things, Jenny; I will be OK." Mariah couldn't hold back any longer. More tears streamed down her face. She was angry at herself for not being able to control her emotions.

"Now what is the matter with you?" Cass asked. "What are you crying for?"

"Just thinking about things, hoping no more happens today," Mariah said, drying her eyes. She was relieved as they turned the corner to see Cass's sisters-in-law playing in the front yard with all the kids in front of Gus and Judy's house.

As they unloaded the truck of small little girls Cass motioned Gus to come over behind the truck. This, Mariah thought, was a dead giveaway that something had happened, and he didn't want the women to know.

"What is going on?" Judy asked. "I have seen that look on Cass's face. Something is up."

"I don't know, he said nothing, but I know better," Mariah told her. "Cub had come to the house to use the phone to call the sheriff and I heard him say 'She is not here.' I'm not sure who he was talking about."

When Cass and Gus were done with their conversation Gus pulled Judy aside and told her what was going on. Judy proceeded to tell the rest of the sisters-in-law and Mariah so the kids would not hear.

Mariah's first thought was Grey had taken her. She shuddered thinking about how the man had grabbed and kneaded her breast to the point of pain until she broke free from him.

Cass must have read her face because he spoke up and

said, "Cub and the sheriff's niece are out trying to find Grey's camp. Maybe he will loan us a couple of his dogs."

Mariah found little comfort in his words. If Grey had taken her, he would have brought her back to make sure she was on time for work, unless something more happened. Liz was a strong-willed woman. Grey would have to prevent her in some way from getting back to work. Mariah shuttered again. She didn't particularly like Liz but didn't want any harm to come to her either.

The day went by and Cass, Mariah, and Jenny stayed most of the day observing how the little girls would get along with the boys. Seemed like the boys were very protective and like big brothers to them. Still Sarah had not talked. She interacted with the others and used hand gestures if she wanted something. At supper the little girl ate very little. When Mariah told Judy, she was very concerned about Sarah, Judy took Mariah's hand and told her this would pass and to give the child some time. The child needs love and lots of hugs, Judy told her. Mariah was amazed at how calmly Judy handled and looked at things. She truly was a great mother, and this was a great place for these little girls to go.

After supper Cass wanted to go home and see why someone had not called him about Liz. As they drove in the driveway the sheriff's truck was there along with Cub's truck. Cass had a sick feeling about this.

"Evening," the sheriff said as they walked up on the porch. "Cass, can I talk to you?"

"Sure. Mariah go on in and put Jenny to bed," Cass said, knowing by the sheriff's tone this was not good.

"Well," the sheriff said with a loud escape of air. "Beth found Grey's camp and Liz was not there. Grey said he had not seen her. I went out and looked around the camp and couldn't see anything that would tell me Liz was there. I asked Grey if he would get his dogs to track Liz in the morning and he agreed. Cub and I went into Liz's apartment and looked around. The lamp in her bedroom was on and everything was on the floor. It looks like drag marks on the carpet where Liz was drug out, we think against her will. Her purse was on the table and the door of the apartment was open. It looks like Liz has been taken against her will."

"Do you have any leads?" asked Cass.

"None," the sheriff answered. "Do you want to go with us in the morning looking for her?"

"I promise to put my feelings for Grey aside if he is going to help find Liz. Yes, I will meet you in town at McCain's," Cass answered. "Cub, what is your feeling on this?" Cass asked Cub, who was in deep thought. Cass's feeling was he was sure Grey had something to do with it and wanted to watch how this played out in the morning.

"Liz would never miss work. She lived for that place. She was a person who had to be around other people. I think we will not see her again," Cub answered. His eyes were thin slants. "Grey, I think, had something to do with it. I am just not sure what he has done with her."

"I feel the same way," the sheriff added as he walked to his truck. "See you in the morning."

Cub also got up to leave. He looked at Cass and turned and said, "I think he is using Liz for bait."

Cass shook his head yes and said back, "My feelings exactly."

CHAPTER TWENTY-THREE

Cass left early before Jenny got up. He instructed Mariah to stay in the house with Wolf and keep the doors locked until he returned. Before he left, he made sure all the doors and windows were locked and asked Mariah if she was going to be OK. Mariah was surprised he asked this but assured him they would be fine with Wolf.

Cass met up with the sheriff and Cub. Grey was already there with three of his dogs ready to go. They started in Liz's bedroom. The dogs were given a piece of Liz's clothing to sniff. When Grey gave the command, the dogs took off bugling down the stairs, pulling Grey behind them to the back of the tavern. Grey yelled at them to "find" and again offered the piece of clothing. The dogs stopped again at the same place in the back of the tavern. They all looked around.

"The trail stops here," Grey announced.

"Well what does that mean?" asked the sheriff, a little put out that this was as far as they got.

Cub stood looking at the garbage bin. He looked up at Cass and said, "I think we need to look in here." He lifted the lid up and peered inside. "Nothing," he announced.

Grey let out a huge big sigh of relief. He offered, "Someone picked her up here and carried her into the alley."

Cass and Cub looked at each other but didn't say anything. It was all Cass could do to not throw Grey in the garbage bin.

"Take the dogs down the alley and see if they can find anything," the sheriff commanded Grey.

Grey walked the dogs out to the alley. They quickly picked

up a scent and again went bugling down the alley, pulling Grey as they went. The rest of the search party followed. The dogs stopped at the back door of Max Pulser's. The sheriff knocked on the door several times but did not get an answer. They all went to the front door and again the sheriff knocked. Max came to the door and opened it.

"What do you guys want?" Max asked as he stood in the doorway with only his pajama bottoms on. His flaming red hair was all a waded mess and had not been washed for a while.

"Have you seen Liz who works at the bar?" the sheriff asked.

"No, the last I saw her was last night. Is she missing?" he asked.

"Can we come in and look around?" asked the sheriff.

"Come in and look around? Why do you think she is here?" Max questioned as the situation had quickly woken him up. "Why would she be here?"

"Well Grey's dogs tracked her to your back door," the sheriff answered. "So, are you going to let us in, or do I have to go get a search warrant?"

"Sure, come on in. I have nothing to hide," Max said and held the door open for them.

Max was a free-spirited man who worked for Henry Hart's logging company when the season was open. The off time he spent drinking mostly and spending time at McCain's. He was a big jolly fellow who Cass thought would never hurt a fly.

As they walked in the front room it was clean and tidy but when they got to the kitchen the stink of dirty dishes and rotten food filled their noses. They quickly turned into the hallway and bedrooms. Next was the basement. It was a maze of junk piled to the ceiling in some places.

"What is all of this about, Sheriff? You say the dogs tracked her here to my back door, but the dogs can't find anything in the house, can they? I had nothing to do with it, I can assure you. If I want Liz for a night, all I do is ask and she will take me up to her apartment. Have you looked there?" Max asked.

Cass knew this to be true because he had been there several times.

"Yes, we looked there. You are not leaving town in the next couple of days for any reason, are you?" the sheriff asked.

"No, no, no plans to," Max said scratching his head. "What the hell is going on here? Got some ghost cat out there killin' people and now a missing person? Not good, not good."

The search party left Max's house and the sheriff thanked Grey for his help. He asked Cass and Cub to come to the sheriff office with him. When they got there the sheriff radioed Beth to spy on Grey and watch him to see if he might be hiding something.

"I know he was relieved when Liz wasn't in the dumpster, but I think that might have been an act. What if he carried Liz to the alley? He could have dragged her up to Max's back door and then carried her away?" Cub asked them both. He didn't really like Liz and tried to avoid her at all cost, but he didn't want anything to happen to her. "I know it was him. I can feel it. And I can feel Liz is in trouble."

There was silence between the three men for a while. Cass knew Liz didn't go out without a fight. Maybe she left some scratches or missing hair on her captor. He just knew Grey had something to do with it.

"I agree with you; that is why I am having Beth see if she can find anything out," the sheriff offered. "I am not sure how he did it or why he would do it. I agree with you about the fact he could be using Liz as bait for that white lion. What do you think, Cass?"

"I agree with both of you. Without proof, the sheriff can't bring charges against him. I myself would love to see him in jail," Cass answered.

The white lion pounced down from his perch on a high ledge. It was almost dark, and he was hungry. He stretched out his full length and yawned. He held his nose up, sniffing the air to see if he could detect any prey, he started to walk, smelling the air as he went. A few hours later he came to a small herd of cattle. These were much larger than the goats he had eaten before, but he singled out a calf by its mother. The night air was still so his presence was not detected by the cattle. Inching up on the calf very slowly, until he was only feet away, finally with a quick jump he landed on the calf. It took only moments for the calf to die. The calf's mother and rest of the herd stampeded away, leaving the lion to eat in peace. He ate until he could eat no more. It returned to its ledge and cleaned his fur of the calf's blood.

When Mariah went to bed, she fell asleep soundly and started to dream. The white lion was walking through the forest. It was like she was watching television. The white lion walked out of the forest into a clearing. Its fur around its mouth, chest, and paws were covered with blood. The large cat stopped and screamed. Mariah watched as the cat walked back into the forest. It looked like now he was dragging something. It looked like Liz from the bar, and she was covered in blood but still alive. Mariah woke up screaming.

Cass woke up to Mariah's screams and rushed to her room. "Mariah! Are you OK? You are having a bad dream," he said when he opened the bedroom door.

"Cass, I dreamed the white lion got Liz from McCain's bar. Man, it was so real. What do you think that means?" she struggled to get the words out of her mouth, taking deep breaths.

Cass sat down on her bed. "Well we know Liz is missing. Are you sure it was her you saw?" Cass asked.

"Yes, it was her," Mariah said, trying to get the vision out of her mind by squeezing her eyes together. "Cass, her hands were tied."

CHAPTER TWENTY-FOUR

Beth walked close to Grey's camp but was careful not to alert the dogs. She climbed a tree to get a better view of the camp. There she sat and watched Grey feed his dogs and make his supper. Didn't look like he was trying to hide anything by what she could see. But after a while she was very surprised to see him walking out of the camp with his gun. She wondered what he was up to this time. He left all his dogs staked and went off by himself.

She climbed down the tree and carefully followed him. After walking for a long time Beth could see him checking trees, he had marked to find his way. She now was convinced he was hiding Liz somewhere and continued to follow him carefully for an hour until he found what he was looking for. His flashlight was looking for something on the ground. She again climbed a tree to see if she could get a better look.

"Lizzy I am here! Want some dinner?" Grey pulled a tarp up, showing a large hole in the earth, probably a bear trap. The tarp had blended into the ground and was hard to see if you were not looking for it. "Lizzy, are you awake?"

"Yeah, get me out of here or I will have you boiled in oil, you son of a bitch," Liz yelled up to him. Beth could tell she was pissed but her voice was cracking.

"No can do. I have plans for you. Gee, the whole town is looking for you, Lizzy. Here is a bag of crackers. Eat them sparingly and I will see you tomorrow," Grey chuckled.

"What the hell kind of plans? What do you want with me?" Beth could tell by Liz's voice she was crying.

"Well tomorrow night you are invited to a party for the big white kitty!" Grey again chuckled. "You like parties, don't you Liz?

"Grey come on. Don't do this. They will know it is you," Liz sobbed, pleading, trying to reason with him.

"Oh, come on, Liz. I promised the big white kitty a little Liz sandwich. Besides, I took the sheriff on a wild goose chase with the dogs today and I am not a suspect any longer!" Grey said as he pulled the tarp back over the hole.

Beth could hear Liz screaming hysterically as Grey walked away. She waited until Grey was far away and climbed down the tree. The night was black, and it was hard to see the beginning of the tarp without a light. Liz screamed again, calling out profanities.

"Liz. Liz, my name is Beth Parker. I am the sheriff's niece. Hang in there and I will try to get you out," Beth told her. Beth had no idea how deep this hole was. She looked around for a log or something she could put down the hole. She found one and cautioned Liz to get up against the side of the hole as she guided the log down the hole. About a foot stuck out of the hole. This told Beth how deep the hole was. Beth removed her jeans and instructed Liz to grab on to one leg and get a good hold on it. Beth instructed her to walk up the log she had rolled into the hole while hanging onto the jeans. When Liz got close enough Beth grabbed her arm and pulled her to safety.

"Thank you, thank you, thank you," Liz said hugging on to Beth, crying hysterically.

"You are welcome but keep it down and let go of my pants so I can put them back on before the bugs get me," Beth said, pulling Liz away from her and quickly putting on her jeans. "Now we have to go quickly and quietly."

"OK, OK." Liz was trying not to cry now and all she could do is sniffle.

"Did you have any shoes on?" Beth asked.

"No, he hit me and knocked me out and took me out of

the bedroom in what I have on, which isn't much. I froze all night," Liz said. She sobbed, crying harder.

"OK. I am going to have to carry you and it is going to be slow going and we will have to go around Grey's camp without alerting his dogs. It will take most of the night. Let's hope the white lion has eaten tonight," Beth said as she slung Liz over her shoulder. "And don't talk unless you have to."

Although Liz was only about one hundred pounds, she slowed Beth down a lot. By the time they got to Beth's camp it was breaking dawn. Beth radioed her uncle telling him she had found Liz.

The sheriff called Cass and Cub telling them to get into town right away.

Once they got to the sheriff's office Liz sat quietly but still crying with a cup of hot coffee in her hand and told them her story in-between sobs. She had left work and walked up the back stairs to her apartment. Moments after she got there, Grey was at her door. She let him in, and she assumed he wanted what most of the men wanted when they came to see her, so she led him into the bedroom. When she went to lay down on the bed Grey hit her, knocking her out, then tied her hands behind her back and stuffed a sock in her mouth. When she came to, he made her walk down the stairs, but she decided she was going to make him carry her. He hit her again and knocked her out. The bruises and black eye proved it. She woke up at the alley and Grey made her walk down the alley by pulling out his knife and told her to walk or he would cut her. She had tried to get away once and this must have been by Max's door. She remembered him hitting her again and knocked her out, she didn't wake up until he lowered her into the hole.

"Cass what I would like to do is go get Grey. Do you want to come with me? It will be light in a bit," said the sheriff. "I'd like both you and Cub to go with me to Grey's camp. I will arrest him, but someone will have to care for the dogs."

Liz now was out of her temporary shock and shouted, "I can't go back to my apartment until Grey is caught. Please, Cass, take me to your house and let me get cleaned up. I can't stay in my apartment tonight, please," she pleaded loudly. "Please?"

Cass quickly thought of Liz and how she would be toward Jenny. "Liz, don't you want to get cleaned up first?"

"No, I can clean up at your house, right?" Liz pleaded now, sobbing harder. "Sheriff's niece can help me get some clothes and shoes. I will probably sleep most of the day being as I couldn't down there in that hole. It was so cold, so cold. I just want to sit in a hot bath and sleep. I promise I will be polite and decent to your nanny and daughter. Please."

Cass decided she was a little different, like the wind had been knocked out of her. He replied with, "OK, but be on your best behavior in front of my daughter. No cursing or lude behavior. Promise me."

A very tearful Liz responded with, "I promise, Cass. Thank you." She continued to cry.

Cass had never seen her cry. Never seen her like this. It was like someone had turned off a switch inside her. He responded, saying softly to Beth, "I will call Mariah and let her know you are coming. Beth, can you take her up to her apartment and pack her some clothes for a while and take her out to the house to clean up and sleep? Grey would have no idea she will be there."

Beth led Liz out the door. The sheriff and Cass waited until Cub got there and they took off to Grey's camp with full intentions of bringing him in and locking him up. When they got to his campsite it had been light for a while, and he had packed up and gone. They spent the rest of the day looking for him throughout the valley but could not find one sign of him or his dogs.

CHAPTER TWENTY-FIVE

Mariah awoke to Wolf barking and someone knocking at the door. She had answered the phone earlier and fell asleep on the couch waiting for the two women. Before opening the door, she looked out to see Beth and Liz. She had never met Beth but did know Liz, so she opened the door. Beth introduced herself and briefly told her what had happened, and that Cass had OK'd Liz to get cleaned up and stay there for a while. Mariah was shocked when she looked Liz over. She was covered in mud and was very quiet, other than her sobbing. Beth helped Liz into the bathroom with Mariah following and said, "Liz, I am going to leave you and go back to town. Will you be OK?"

Liz answered, still sobbing, "Yes, thank you."

Beth looked at Mariah and said, "If you need anything, call the sheriff's office. They will get a message to us."

Mariah turned on the tub and got towels out. While she was doing this Liz stood there, sobbing more loudly. Mariah went to leave the bathroom, but Liz softly grabbed her arm and asked, "Please, can you help me?"

"Sure," Mariah said. "Lay back and I will wash your hair first." She helped Liz out of her clothes and into the tub. Mariah had done this for her mother many times. It concerned her Liz just sat there letting Mariah wash her and continued to cry. She had numerous bruises and scrapes. Her fingernails were broken, and the black dirt was caked under them. Mariah felt sorry for her. Liz allowed her to cut and clean her nails. After she bathed Liz Mariah helped her out of the tub and into the clothes Beth had brought in. Liz continued to whimper.

"He was going to feed me to the lion," Liz said as Mariah combed out her hair. "I could have died."

Mariah said nothing, just placed her hand on Liz's shoulder to console her. She combed and dried Liz's hair and helped her into the bed of one of the spare bedrooms. Mariah closed the door and went to look in on Jenny. She was still asleep, so Mariah picked up Liz's clothes and threw them in the washing machine. Memories of Grey gave her an ill feeling and if he could bring Liz to the state she was in, Mariah could only imagine what he was capable of.

Liz slept most of the day and didn't come downstairs until supper was cooking. She meekly stepped into the kitchen where Mariah and Jenny were making biscuits. "Thank you," Liz quietly said. "I'm not sure how to ever repay you and Cass. You are very kind."

"Are you hungry?" Mariah asked. Mariah could see how red and swollen her eyes were from all the crying she had done. She had large purple bruising under her eye and cheek. Even with all the bruising she really was pretty with no makeup on.

"Yes, very. Thank you," Liz answered.

Cass came in from outside and was glad to see Liz was up. She was different. He felt sorry for her and said, "Liz, you are welcome to stay as long as you need to. I do want you to know Grey is no longer in the valley and I think you will be safe."

"Can I stay for a day or two?" she answered. "I just don't want to be alone right now."

"Sure," Cass said. "Can you tell me where Grey planned to capture the lion?"

"I am not sure where he was going to place me, but he was going to tie me up and leave me," Liz said and started crying again.

"Liz, we will talk about this at another time. Mariah why don't you set the table," Cass said.

"I need to call work and see if I can return to work on Thursday. Today is Tuesday, right?" Liz asked. She was very worried she might have lost her job.

"Go ahead and give him a call. He is very worried about you and doesn't know you have been found," Cass said.

They finished dinner and sat out on the screened-in porch watching the sunset. The trees seemed greener, Mariah thought. The lake was calm and looked like glass. They sat in silence and marveled in the beauty.

Mariah stood up with Jenny in her arms and said, "I'm going to put Jenny to bed and take a shower." During her shower she shuddered when she thought of Grey wanting to use Liz as bait. She couldn't understand how someone could do this to another human being.

Later she came back downstairs to find Liz had gone back to bed. Cass now was on the back windowed porch. She curled up with a book Doc had brought her on her bed. She had never felt so safe. Soon she had fallen asleep while reading and quickly went into a dream state.

She was walking through a forest with lots of underbrush and tall trees that hid the sun. The leaves and ferns were a brilliant green and wet with dew. Her clothing was wet, and it was difficult for her to avoid prickly plants that caught her clothing. She walked for what seemed like a long time and soon came upon a clearing. She looked out over it and saw Nooka sitting on a rock. Blood trickled down her neck. Mariah walked up to her and took her hand. Nooka got up and they both went to walk over to the forest again. Mariah helped Nooka through the forest and found a road. They walked for a while until Cass came by and they got into his pickup. No one said anything and Mariah awoke.

Panic seized her. Did this mean Nooka was going to be lost in the forest? She went downstairs and walked out onto the back porch where Cass was still sitting. She told him of her dream. It was past midnight, but Cass called Cub to go check on his great-grandmother anyway. Mariah went back to bed but didn't get much sleep. The dream, what did it mean? She wondered if Nooka had the same dream.

The large cat awoke with emptiness in his stomach. He stretched, yawned, and jumped down off the ledge. He tipped his head up as he walked and sniffed the air. He came upon Beth's camp. He walked around it, smelling her scent. He approached her tent and continued to get closer. Beth was inside sleeping. She woke up with a strange feeling and sat straight up. She listened and couldn't hear anything but seemed to sense something. Suddenly she heard one of her men yelling, "Beth!"

She grabbed her pants and slid them on quickly and unzipped her tent and quickly stepped out. She saw one of her men standing by his tent with his gun pointed at the something next to her tent. "Tom, what is it?" She swung her head around to see the lion, which seemed to be frozen watching her, "Don't shoot, please." She quietly asked. "Don't you think it is strange it didn't run when you called out my name?"

"Yes. What does it want?" asked William, one of the other men in her camp.

"I am not sure, but I don't think it means any harm so, don't shoot." Liz stared into the eyes of the cat for a time and soon the cat turned and ran into the undergrowth.

"That was awesome!" Beth said with excitement. "Tom, where were you sitting to see him come into the camp?

"I saw the flash of white and thought it was the cat but was not sure. He looked right at me and walked around your tent. It took all I had to not shoot. He kept getting closer and closer to the tent and that is when I yelled, hoping to scare him off or at least away from your tent. But he didn't move. He continued to sniff the air until you came out. Do you think he might be rabid?" asked Tom, visually shaken. "I just don't understand why he didn't scatter."

"Well, I guess we better be cautious; it is not normal. He acts like he has no fear of us," Beth said, hating the fact. "We can't hunt him tonight so William will replace you, Tom, on lookout." She turned and went back into her tent. She lay there remembering the yellow eyes of the cat staring back at her. She concluded this was a very strange animal. They had to be careful. First thing in the morning she and her men would track the animal from the camp and hopefully they could dart it and get it in a cage. With Grey out of the picture she was sure this would not be a problem.

The large cat walked away from the campsite. He had looked the humans in the eye and decided they were not a threat to him when he saw Beth; he remembered her scent. He left their camp; his curiosity was satisfied, and he now went on to hunt again and soon found a doe deer which he easily killed, ravishing most of it. It dragged the deer under the underbrush, hiding the remains when he was full and satisfied.

CHAPTER TWENTY-SIX

Cub answered Cass's call and quickly jumped out of bed and dressed. He drove quickly to his great-grandmother's house and knocked. There was no answer, so he knocked louder and yelled for his great-grandmother. Still he could not raise her. He listened and could only hear the night. He opened the door and turned the lights on. His great-grandmother lay on her side, unconscious on the floor. He rushed to her and checked her pulse. She was still alive, and he could feel a very weak pulse. He cradled her against him and found she had a gash on the back of her head, which was still bleeding. Cub took off his shirt and held it over the wound. He ran to the next cabin and called Doc to come to his great-grandmothers. Next, he called Cass who said he would be right there.

Cub again cradled his great-grandmother while he looked around for some clue as to what had happened. It looked like someone had been here. Who could have done this? He was sure Grey had left the valley but if he drove here someone would have recognized and would hear his loud vehicle. He could see things were thrown around and furniture was broken but couldn't see what had been used to hit his great-grandmother from where he was sitting on the floor. He didn't want to leave her until Doc came.

Doc arrived quickly and assessed Nooka's wound. He told Cub she would need stitches and explained to Cub he would have to hold his great-grandmother while he stitched her up. Nooka didn't come to. Doc suggested Cub put her on the couch.

Doc let out a long breath and said, "Cub, call the sheriff and let him know there was a break in and assault on your great-grandmother. Do you see anything missing?"

They both looked at each other. Cub shot up from the chair he was setting in and ran to the other room. He returned with an angry look and said, "The white lion pelt is gone." Now he was sure it was Grey. Anger mounted and he took a deep breath. "It has to be Grey," Cub said through clenched teeth, his rage very apparent.

Doc patted him on the back, trying to console him and calm him down. He had never seen Cub so angry.

Soon Cass pulled up to Nooka's, about the same time the sheriff arrived. Doc and Cub met them on the porch and explained what they thought had happened. "Do you think Grey is back in the valley?" Cub asked the sheriff. "He was about the only one that showed an interest in it. His van was so loud someone would have been alerted."

"I guess he could have. We all looked for him in the valley and just assumed he was gone for good. I guess he could have parked far away and walked here so no one could hear him. Daybreak we will send out a search party to see if we can track him. Cub, would you be our tracker?" the sheriff asked.

"Yes, I will help. I will get Jamie to come and stay with great-grandmother. Doc is she going to wake up?" Cub asked. He swallowed hard and looked down before he looked at Doc, trying to control his anger and rage.

"We will have to give her some time," Doc answered again, patting Cub on the back.

Doc stayed with Nooka until Jamie got there and Cass and Cub were out most of the day until late afternoon tracking Grey. But Grey had eluded them and was nowhere to be found.

Cass drove home in deep thought. When he arrived home, he slowly climbed the steps to the porch and saw the front door lock had been broken. Fear jolted through his body. He rushed in to see Wolf lying on the floor, shot but still alive. A chill went up Cass's spine. He ran through the downstairs and when he got to Jenny's room, he found Liz tied up and gagged.

Cass quickly untied Liz. "I think he took them!" Liz said after coughing a bit. "Grey broke in and grabbed them and tied them up. I hid under Jenny's bed, but he found me and tied me up. I heard him say they were going with him."

Liz now was crying but Cass had little time to console her. He quickly called Doc. "Doc, Wolf has been shot but he isn't dead. Can you come out look at him? Grey took Mariah and Jenny. It would be dark soon. I have to go find them," he stated, his voice cracking.

"Cass, I will be right there. Is Liz still there?" Doc asked.

"Yes. She is a little shaken but OK. Doc, I have to go." Cass quickly hung up and left. He was not sure where to start but thought maybe he could get some help from Beth.

Doc quickly jumped in his car and went to the sheriff's office where he was happy to see Cub there also. He quickly explained to both what was going on.

"I will go find Cass and help him," Cub stated. "If I find Grey, he will wish he never came to our valley. He did this to great-grandmother to pull Cass away from the house."

The sheriff stood there shaking his head and asked, "Cub, can I come with you? We can take the patrol truck. I really think I would have better luck finding Grey with you."

Cub and the sheriff followed Doc out the door. Doc drove to Cass's to save wolf. Cub and the sheriff went to find Mariah and Jenny.

"Cass is going to be furious. Hell knows what he is capable of when it comes to Jenny," the sheriff commented while heading south out of town. "I am sure if we don't find Grey first Cass will take it into his own hands to make Grey pay." His thoughts were with Cass. He must be at wits end, capable of murdering Grey.

Grey unloaded Mariah first and tied her to a tree. Mariah wondered where Grey had found this different vehicle. Next, he got Jenny out of the truck. She was quietly crying and kept her large blue eyes on Mariah. Grey sat her down and untied her hands. He said, "Now I will leave your hands untied if you are good. But if you try to run away, I will send my dogs after you." Jenny continued to look at Mariah. Grey grabbed Jenny's chin and roughly turned it toward him. "Do you understand?" he yelled.

Jenny defiantly looked Grey in the eye and nodded her head yes. She looked around but could see no dogs. She listened. No sound of any dogs. "Will you let me go home? I will be good," Jenny begged.

"No, you're not going anywhere," he answered smartly and went to get firewood from the back of the tent. When he returned Jenny was gone. "Where did she go?" he demanded from Mariah.

Mariah smiled but didn't answer. "God damn," he cursed. "She'll be back when it gets dark or maybe the white lion eats her. Either way I'm not going to waste any more time worrying about it," he said as he busied himself making a fire.

Jenny ran through the undergrowth as fast as she could, not sure of where she was going but she wanted to get as far away from that awful man with the bad breath as she could. Her hands hadn't been tied so she easily ran between the underbrush. She knew her dad would be looking for her and Mariah. Boy, he was really going to hurt Grey. She hoped the man would not hurt Mariah and hoped her dad got there first. This thought stopped her in her tracks. She had to go back and try to help Mariah. Slowly, Jenny turned around and walked back to just outside the camp. It was dark now. Grey sat at the fire and Mariah was a few feet away, still tied to the tree. It smelled like Grey was cooking something. She tried to think how she could get behind Mariah and untie her without Grey seeing her. She would wait and watch him before doing anything.

Grey looked directly at Mariah and asked, "Would you like some beans? Your little brat is going to miss this great meal I have cooked."

"No," answered Mariah. She was starting to get chilled and wondered how far Jenny would get before she also got cold. The thought of her out there by herself with the white lion roaming around sickened her. "Please let me go. I am no use to you."

"Sure, you are. I am going to use you for bait. The white lion will love you," Grey said, finishing his food and quickly putting out the fire. "I got to get going. I am going to pack up and leave you here. I will be a few hundred yards away so when you scream, I can come running and shoot the animal. I will let him eat a little first." He got in the new vehicle, turned it around, and drove away.

Jenny couldn't believe he was leaving. When he was gone, she ran out of the bushes and untied Mariah.

"Jenny!" she cried. "Oh, thank you. We must get away from here and be very quiet. Quickly now, understand?"

"Yes," Jenny said, smiling up at Mariah. "Let's go."

They ran through the undergrowth as fast as they could for hours. Jenny was totally worn out. "Let's rest a while," Jenny said. "He can never find us."

"He can track us. We need to keep moving and try to find a place that is safe," Mariah told her. "The dogs will find us quickly. Here, get on my back."

They finally came to a dirt road. Mariah looked both ways, not sure which way to go. She closed her eyes and prayed that whichever way she chose would be the right way. She chose to go left. Soon she could see a light. She started getting closer and could see the house. She started running with Jenny on her back. When she got to the house, she ran up the front stairs and pounded on the door loudly. An old man and his wife came to the door and opened it slowly. "Who are you and what are you doing out this time of night?" the old man asked.

Mariah explained their ordeal and asked him to call the sheriff. His wife had them both wrapped in a blanket and gave them hot tea. By the time Mariah had finished telling them the story of the kidnapping Jenny had fallen asleep in her lap.

The sheriff and Cub finally got there, but neither of them asked them to talk about their ordeal. The car ride back to Cass's house was quiet. Mariah thought of Wolf and the fact that he was shot and probably dead. This saddened her and she let the tears flow.

"Mariah, we will take you home and Doc will stay with you until we find Cass. He went out by himself looking for you two," the sheriff told her. "We are going to find Beth and hopefully she has seen him."

When they got back to Cass's house Cub took Jenny into her room and put her to bed. Doc was sitting by Wolf on the floor, who had a large bandage around his middle. Mariah got tearful again; she thought for sure Wolf had been killed when Grey shot him.

Mariah asked, pointing at Wolf, "I hope he is all right. Can I pet him?"

Doc noticed how tired Mariah looked. As they both petted Wolf Doc said, "Yes, he will be OK. I had to dig a bullet out of him, so he is sedated. He will be fine. Are you OK?"

Mariah just noticed all her bug bites were now itching and looked at her arms with many scratches. "Yes, I am OK—lots of bites. I didn't look Jenny over, but I can image she has just as many." She now was in full-blown tears. "This man has got to be caught. No one is safe."

Cub came out of Jenny's room and asked her, "Can you tell me where he took you?"

"I am not sure. I think west of here, but it was dark, and he made several turns. We walked a long way. Poor Jenny! I have to tell you she is very brave to stay out in the undergrowth and come back to untie me," Mariah said between sobs.

"Well get some sleep. I am going to look for Cass," Cub told her.

Doc stayed at Cass's and instructed the sheriff to call him if he needed anything. He told Cass he would have to check on Nooka in the morning. The sheriff got a hold of Beth on the radio. She was with Cass and he was on his way home. Beth would continue to look for Grey.

CHAPTER TWENTY-SEVEN

Cass was relieved to hear both Mariah and Jenny were OK. It was like a large weight had been lifted off his chest. When he found out they had walked through the forest he was fuming. They could have been easy pickings if the lion had been in the area. He was still going to find Grey in the morning if Beth hadn't found him and make him wish he had never come here. He had heard the conversation Beth had with the sheriff on their radios. Cass was sure the sheriff really wanted Beth to find Grey but to not do anything until he could arrest him.

Before Beth got off the radio, he asked her to have the sheriff let him know also. The thought that Grey taking the white pelt from Nooka might have been a ploy to get him out of the house so he could take Mariah and Jenny. He never dreamed Grey would be that brazen.

At the same time Grey had just found out Mariah was gone from the tree. He really didn't have any dogs with him there, so he decided to get out of the area quickly. He could not believe the little brat had been able to untie Mariah. Oh, he will get his revenge, he thought to himself. As he drove away, he made another plan.

The white lion awoke at dawn. He could smell the familiar scent of the human Beth. He scanned the valley from the ledge he slept on. He couldn't see her but knew she was close. He wasn't hungry so he stayed on his ledge.

Beth had looked most of the night for a sign of a campfire Grey might have built to fend off the cool night air but wasn't able to see any. This was quite a distance from where she had found Liz. She had already looked in that area and couldn't find any trace of Grey. Beth couldn't hear any dogs. Grey must have taken his dogs somewhere to be kept while he took Nooka's pelt and kidnapped the girls. Where? she thought. Not familiar with the area she radioed the sheriff and asked him where he thought Grey would have taken the dogs, but the sheriff had no idea. He told her there were many old logging cabins high in the mountains, but he doubted Grey would know about them. He was sure Grey would have had to go out of the valley to get anyone to care for his dogs. Her guess now was Grey also had left the valley last night. He probably knew of all the people who would be after him. She sighs deeply, thinking it was going to be hard to find him now.

Cass had awaked early. He looked in on Jenny, but she was still sleeping. He went into the kitchen where he saw Mariah making coffee. "Are you OK?" asked Cass. He could see the scratches and bug bites on her arms.

"Yes, just a lot of bug bites. I am sure Jenny has a lot of them too. I will have Doc bring us out something today to put on them."

Liz came into the kitchen and hugged Mariah. "I am so sorry." Mariah patted her hand. "Please let me help make breakfast." They worked alongside each other, both smiling.

Cass went into Jenny's room. He couldn't stand it any longer. He had to find out if she was OK.

"Hey, little one," he said softly while he shook her shoulder. "Mariah has breakfast started. I bet you are hungry."

Slowly Jenny opened her eyes and smiled at Cass, "Yes, Daddy, I saved Mariah last night." She quickly scrambled out from under the covers to hug him. "Ouch, look at all my bug bites and scratches!" she exclaimed proudly.

"Yes, you are very brave. Doc is going to bring out some medicine to put on your bites and scratches. I am so sorry that bad man took you," Cass said, grabbing and hugging her tight.

"Daddy, I think he is a very bad man and I told him you would be coming for him!" she exclaimed as Cass set her down. She rubbed her stomach and proclaimed, "I am starving!"

When they entered the kitchen, Mariah had already made eggs and toast and soon Jenny was talking about everything else except the kidnapping. Doc came in just in time to eat breakfast with them.

He brought medicine for Mariah and Jenny. While putting the medicine on Mariah's arm he said, "Nooka is awake. She confirmed Grey was the one that hit her on the head and took the pelt. I think he took the back roads from Nooka's to here. It was a well-planned kidnapping. It almost worked but was foiled by a little five-year-old girl!" Doc laughed his belly laugh. "But we still need to be very careful. Only three days until the church social. I am very worried. Now both the white lion and Grey need to be found," he said quietly to Cass.

"Don't worry, Doc. We will have men with rifles guarding all the folk. I doubt if the white lion will come close, but I am sure Grey would be the one that can ruin the day," Cass said, hoping to himself this was true, but the white lion had hunted during the day and grabbed the Native American child.

They all had just sat down to eat when someone knocked at the door. Cass asked, "Are we expecting anyone else?" He opened the door to find Beth. "Come in, we were just sitting down to eat breakfast. Let us set you a plate."

"That would be great," Beth answered. "I wanted to let you know I couldn't find any trace of Grey. I think he again left the valley. I am pretty sure he has taken his dogs somewhere out of the valley. I am not sure anyone here would be interested in keeping them for him. He must have had a different car—one that was much quieter."

Mariah told them he did have a different vehicle and it was red, but she didn't know what kind it was.

Cass nodded his head yes. "I agree. If he had the dogs with him, he could have set them free and they could have tracked Mariah and Jenny," he stopped suddenly and looked at Jenny. "Did you see any dogs?"

"I knew he didn't have any dogs, Daddy. He warned me if I ran away, he would send his dogs after me. But I couldn't hear or see any dogs. That is why I came back and untied Mariah," Jenny said nonchalantly.

All of them looked at each other but didn't say anything. They all knew how lucky Mariah and Jenny had been to escape.

"I hope you are still going to try and get the white lion," Cass said to Beth.

"Yes, I plan on going to the west side of the valley. It is like looking for a needle in a haystack. But now with Grey out of the picture I can give my full attention to it," Beth said, finishing her breakfast quickly. She thanked Cass and everyone for having her for breakfast and left, refueled to hunt again.

The white lion awoke on the ledge and looked out over the valley. Slowly he got up and stretched. He was hungry. He jumped from the ledge and took off, sniffing the air. He came upon a small doe and quickly killed and pulled it under the bushes and devoured it quickly. Yes, the valley was a great food source for him.

CHAPTER TWENTY-EIGHT

Grey had not left the valley. Days before he had gone far into the forest up the mountain in search of a hideout. This was an area where few people ventured. Roads were very poor, and very few people lived up there. He ran across a cabin inhabited by old Charlie Harris. Charlie was ninety years old and almost blind. He was a hermit, rarely had any company and lived off the land. He was very hostile to Grey when he opened the door. But Grey pushed the door of the cabin open and hit Charlie over the head a little too hard. The blow had killed Charlie instantly. Grey buried him in the backyard. Grey also could not afford for his remaining dogs to make any noise giving his hideout away, so he shot them.

Grey had gone back to the cabin after he found Mariah had vanished. He was pretty sure the lion would have gotten them, or the elements had. He knew Cass would be furious and would stop at nothing to find him. Grey had spent most of night thinking out a plan. Old Charlie had a Jeep in the shed and plenty of gasoline in cans. It looked like maybe the gas might have been intended for the generator, but Grey put some of it in the Jeep.

He would somehow now attempt to kidnap someone else and use them for bait. He would have to do some spying. The first place would be Cass's house. He would wait until nightfall. He had to make sure the woman and child had not made it back.

Nightfall came. Grey hid the Jeep about a mile away and grabbed his gun and walked through the forest. He boldly crept up next to Cass's house and looked through the window. He could see Cass, Mariah, and Jenny sitting in the front room. He could easily shoot Cass and have his way with Mariah and use the little girl as bait. Also, he was shocked to see he had not killed that damn dog. Well, now he knew the girls were alive. How on earth did they make it through the forest? Grey walked back to the Jeep, angry they both were still alive. He drove to town and past Liz's upstairs apartment and saw that lights were on. Was she back at work, he wondered? He drove to McCain's and parked in the parking lot to wait and observe. He waited for what seemed like an eternity. Finally, he saw Liz walk out on her way home. This was what he was waiting for. It looked like things were back to normal. He would go back to the cabin to plan. He knew the church social was Sunday. The church social would have lots of people coming and going. This would be an ideal time to snatch someone.

Back at Cass's Mariah had gone to bed early and fallen into a deep sleep. She was flying over the lake and landed in a clearing just over the bridge. She started walking and soon could see movement ahead of her. She stopped to see Cass and Jenny just getting out of the truck. She walked faster but they kept getting further away. She now was running toward them. The white lion jumped out in front of her. His yellow eyes stared at her, his tail whipping back and forth. She was somehow not scared for herself but for Cass and Jenny.

Suddenly the white lion turned and ran toward Cass and Jenny. Mariah took off and ran after it. It was getting closer and closer to Cass and Jenny. Mariah's heart was pounding, and she was gasping for breath. In a quick flash Beth jumped out in front of her and Mariah woke up. She was hyperventilating and ran down the stairs, unlocked the door, and went out on the front porch.

Cass had fallen asleep on the couch and was awakened by Mariah opening the door. Slowly he moved toward the door, finally realizing it had to be Mariah. He walked out on the porch and saw Mariah gasping for breath. She turned to him and said, "Cass my dream, my dream was so real. Grey was after you and Jenny. I was running and you both were getting further away. Beth jumped out in front of me and I woke up." She looked at him and added, "You have got to be careful. You have to keep Jenny safe." She started sobbing uncontrollably.

Cass went to her and hugged her. Slowly he said, "It is going to be OK. Grey hasn't been in the valley for days. He won't come close; I can assure you." Cass was very aware of how good she felt against him. He held her until she quit sobbing. "Now we should go inside—don't want to give the white lion any easy targets." He slowly drew away from her and pushed her easily in the small of her back toward the door. Just then there was a loud scream very close to them. It was the white lion again; both froze. Slowly they turned around to see the lion only feet away from the porch again. Cass quickly forced Mariah into the house, shutting the door behind them.

"Again, we were very lucky," Cass said slowly. "Go to bed." He wiped his hand over his face. Why was this lion again so close to the house? It was like it was stalking them.

Mariah felt exhausted and never really feared the white lion being so close. She was calm now and went to bed, still feeling Cass's arms around her. She had wondered several times what this would feel like. She had only good dreams the rest of the night.

Cass didn't go to his gun shelf and get a gun to shoot off; somehow, he felt unthreatened tonight by the white lion. He wondered why this was. He had never seen a mountain lion come this close to man and couldn't understand why but right now he didn't fear him. Maybe it was because he was with Mariah. He went to bed remembering how she felt in his arms and how good she smelled. He fell asleep quickly.

The white lion had smelled Grey in the forest and had followed the scent to Cass's. When the white lion saw the humans on the porch, he was drawn to them. When they went back into the house he walked back into the forest. Hunger was now on his mind and he sniffed the air. A small deer had wandered too close to the cat. The white lion had crouched in the undergrowth, slowly stalking toward the deer. When the deer was close enough, he pounced, nearly missing the deer, but was able to swipe the back legs, causing the animal to fall. Quickly the cat found the deer's neck and with a single bite hit the jugular and the deer died quickly. When the cat was satisfied the deer no longer would try to get away, he fed until he could eat no more and climbed onto a rock ledge to clean itself and soon fell asleep.

Beth heard the cat's scream and turned toward the sound. She had camped close to Cass's house and was unaware of how close Grey had been to the house and her camp.

The day of the church social came without any further incidences. Mariah had set her alarm to get up early to cook dishes they were taking to the social. When she had the food cooked and prepared, she went to the back porch and looked out over the lake. It was calm without a ripple in the water. She could hear the early morning birds singing their song. The trees were thick and green, and she marveled at how beautiful it was around her. Mariah remembered the dreams she'd had in Kansas of green trees and mountains. She frequently thought of how her life had been in Kansas and how different it was now. The family in Seattle probably had hired someone else to be their nanny by now. The thought of not having any place to go now frightened her. She hoped Cass would allow her to keep being Jenny's nanny. The child was so sweet, and Mariah had become so attached to her. She wasn't sure she could ever leave her. Remembering how badly the poor little one looked the first morning Mariah met her and what she looked like now warmed her heart. Jenny had put on a little weight and always had clothes neatly laundered and hair well kept. Also, Cass's mom and dad and all of Cass's brothers had made her feel so accepted. With a big sigh Mariah got up and went into the kitchen to start breakfast. When she entered the kitchen, Cass was pouring a cup of coffee.

"Good morning!" Mariah said. She quickly went over to the counter and started breakfast. She was always uncomfortable now with Cass. Just his presence in a room made her heart beat faster. "Is Jenny up?" she asked, continuing her tasks. She avoided looking at him most of the time now because when their eyes met a bolt went through her, making her weak-kneed. She wondered how this could be when he obviously didn't care for her.

"Not yet, good morning," Cass said, looking out the window. He also spent very little time alone in the same room as Mariah. He didn't trust his body not to betray him. He was falling for her and he knew it. He couldn't let this happen.

Jenny came running into the room and quickly went over and hugged her dad and then went to hug Mariah. "Good morning!" she exclaimed with excitement. "Mariah, it smells wonderful in here. Can I have one of the rolls you made?" Her eyes were bright and happy."

"May I have a roll?" Mariah corrected her. "Yes, you may have one. I will get you some jelly."

After breakfast Cass went outside and walked the perimeter of the house like he did each morning. He was about to go in the house when his eyes focused on a footprint by the side of his house. With much curiosity he bent and examined the print and was sure it was a man's print. It was fresh, very fresh. It had to be last night when whoever it was came close enough to peer into the window. The print was not his and was too small to be Cub's or Doc's. A cold chill ran through him. It had to be Grey's.

Cass entered the house and went directly to the phone. He called Cub to come over and look at the print. When Cub got there, he told Cass Beth had been camped just about a mile west of Cass's house. Cub called the sheriff to contact Beth to see if she had been around the house the previous night. The sheriff confirmed Beth had not been out of her camp. Cub knew the print was too small to be Beth's and told Cass this before the sheriff had called back. Beth wanted to come over and view the print herself and shortly showed up at the door.

"Cass, I am sure it is Grey's print. I have tracked him before. I am going to see if I can tell where he came out of the forest and see if I can see how he got here," stated Beth. "I would just like to know where he has been for all these days without us knowing he is in the valley." She left quickly, shaking her head. Damn Grey. How could he be so brazen? She quickly found where he had entered from the forest and tracked him about a half a mile until it looked like he had walked up to the road. He must have had a quiet vehicle. The van was noisy, and Cass could have heard it start and stop. Sound traveled well in the valley, just like the cat screams. She would continue to look for Grey.

Time came for Cass, Mariah, and Jenny to leave for the social. All the food was packed in the truck safely and Mariah had dressed Jenny in a cute pink dress. They piled in the truck and took off, leaving Wolf in the house. Cass locked the door. He thought as he was locking the door about how he never had to do this before Grey.

When they got to the churchyard it was packed with people and tables filled with food. People were standing, sitting on blankets, lawn chairs, and some just sitting on the grass. Little kids were playing games and running all around chasing each other. Mariah smiled to herself. Nothing like this was ever done in Kansas. Church socials were done in the church basement. Most of the time the children were told to sit and behave, but this was so much better.

Pasture Bob did a quick sermon before eating.

Mariah sat the dishes she had made on the tables and saw Carrie sitting close by.

"Jenny lets go over and talk with Carrie to see how she is feeling," Mariah said, taking Jenny's hand and leading her toward Carrie, where they sat down on her blanket to talk. "How are you feeling, Carrie?" Mariah asked when they sat down.

"Really good, am healing very well," exclaimed Carrie. "Doc says I am going to be just fine. I will have several scars, but they don't show unless I wear a low blouse or dress—which I don't plan on wearing!" she added.

Carrie and Mariah talked with each other until it was time to eat. More tables were set up to eat on and everyone enjoyed trying to eat a little of everything. Mariah rubbed her stomach and said to Jenny, "I am so full I am going to burst!" She laughed and Jenny nodded her head with a mouth full of cherry pie.

Mariah spied Nooka sitting in a lawn chair and said, "Looks like Nooka is here. Would you like to go over with me to see how she is doing?"

"Oh yes. I see May is there. Can I play with her?" Jenny asked while they walked over to Nooka.

Jamie was by Nooka's side; she greeted them warmly. Nooka looked so tiny in the chair. Jamie sat on a blanket next to her with Nooka's great-great-granddaughter, May.

"Hi May. Want to go play?" Jenny asked. She walked over to May and took her hand.

"Stay close. Don't wonder off," Mariah warned. "Nooka, how have you been?" she asked.

"Very good, I am gaining strength every day," Nooka answered her. "I wonder how you are. The dream you told me about the other day has not happened yet. Please be careful."

"I will. Did Cub bring you?" Mariah asked.

"Yes. I wanted to come, and when this is over, I would like you to come to my house and we will talk," Nooka stated. "Cub can take you home when we are done."

Mariah went over to Cass and told him she was going to go over to Nooka's and Cub would take her home. Cass told her he would take Jenny home.

When Jamie, Cub, and Mariah, got to Nooka's, they made Nooka comfortable on the couch. Nooka told them all to sit around her. She had to tell them something she had never told anyone. But first she asked, "Do you have a question, Mariah?"

Mariah asked what ritual she needed to go through.

"Yes, this is what we are going to talk about. Jamie has told you, Mariah, you would have a ritual to go through. Sorry, but it is the truth you must know from me and not a ritual. There is something I must tell all of you about my children."

"Out of curiosity, how many children do you have, Nooka?" Mariah asked. "Please tell me something about your family?" Mariah was now very curious on why she would be included.

Nooka answered, "I had one boy named Namue, who married Yamhas. They had three children: two boys and a girl. My granddaughter Minue went to our ancestors two years ago. She was a beautiful woman. My one son Kanue left the tribe about twenty-five years ago. He worked in construction, somewhere in Nebraska. I never heard from him again. I will give you the name he took after he left the tribe later. My grandson Nacan is still alive and is Cub's father. I have lived here for all my life. This is where I will die soon," Nooka said.

This alarmed all of them.

"I hope not for a while!" Mariah commented, smiling at Nooka.

"Mariah. You wonder how and why you are here and why you were the chosen one to rid the valley of the white lion. I will tell you I saw you born in my dreams. I saw you as a child, and your life in Kansas. The reason why is Kanue, my grandson, is your father. His name he took when he left the tribe was Joseph Glory. Kanue is my grandson, and you are his firstborn child," Nooka explained and waited for all of their reactions.

Mariah took a quick intake of air. She was at a loss for words. Her tears started to flow.

None said a word so Nooka went on, "The white lion comes only when he is needed. We need him now for something."

"Great Grandmother, why did you not tell us this?" a very shocked Cub asked. "I could have gone for her and brought her back to you."

Nooka sighed and explained, "The spirits tell me your father was with your mother only one time in Omaha where they met one night in a bar. He died in an accident soon after this. They were not married. Your mother was not able to tell Kanue of you because she didn't know she was pregnant yet. So, he didn't know of you before he died. Your mother moved back to Kansas with her family. Did she ever speak of your father?"

"Only that his name was Joseph Glory," Mariah said, visibly in full blown tears as they streamed down her face. "She thought he left her. My mother didn't know his family, so she moved back to her family and I was born in Kansas. She raised me by herself," Mariah said swallowing hard, still in shock. "I have a family." More tears started down her cheeks. "Cub, we are cousins," she said, sobbing.

"You have many," Cub said. "Now I understand why the spirits picked you, Mariah.

Both Jamie and Cub hugged Mariah and welcomed her into their family. They both said they would teach her the history of the tribe.

Nooka said, "Now we must talk about the white lion. You will be the only one who can call it so it can be killed. It will be drawn to you. Killing it will be the only way to rid the mountain of the cat."

"Kill it? I have never killed anything before in my life. How can I kill it?" Mariah asked.

Nooka's withered hand squeezed Mariah's. "The great spirit of the mountain will guide you and this will happen soon. When it does you must skin the cat and display it where all can see. Now I must rest, and Cub will take you home." Nooka leaned back into the couch and closed her eyes.

Mariah watched the old woman as she slowly drifted off

to sleep. She was confused about all Nooka had revealed to her. How would she be able to end the life of a beautiful animal like that? Some sadness crossed her heart, but then she remembered Nooka's story. She smiled to herself. She had a family! Cub, Mariah, and Jamie sat on Nooka's front porch for a while as they visited about the family tree and some of the tribal customs.

Mariah thought of her father while Cub took her home. He had really passed away before she was born. Too bad she could not tell her mother he did not leave her. She had found out so many things about her family tonight. Her heart was full.

The white lion climbed down off the cliff. He was restless. Something pulled him to go to the other side of the valley, over by the larger mountain, to a place few people went to. He slowly walked below the underbrush, stopping to sniff the air. He was not hungry. An unknown force made him venture further up the mountain. Here the trees had never been cut and the forest was thicker.

CHAPTER TWENTY-NINE

Cass and Jenny packed up what was left of the dishes and food they had brought and put them in the truck. They said goodbye to all his brothers and their families. Cass's mom and dad hugged them and told them to come over when they could. Logging would be starting soon, and family time would be limited.

Cass drove home, thinking of the dream Mariah had. The hair on this neck stood up. Jenny and he were alone in the truck. He shook his head, laughing at himself. It was broad daylight; nothing was going to happen.

Cub and Mariah left Nooka's and drove past the church-yard to see everyone had left. It had been a glorious day, Mariah thought. As Cub turned the corner almost to Cass's house, he stomped on the breaks. They both looked at each other in shock. Cass's truck was pulled to the side of the road. Mariah's heart went into her throat. Something was wrong. Cub told Mariah to stay in the truck but when Jenny's little head popped up in the windshield Mariah jumped out of the truck and ran to her. Mariah opened the door and fell backward by the quick movement of Jenny jumping in her arms. Cub caught them both. Jenny sobbed hysterically and said, "The mean man took daddy. He took him!" Jenny screamed. She had been crying, it looked like, for a long time. Mariah held her and asked, "Tell me what happened and which way they went."

"The mean man told me to stay in the truck or he would hurt my daddy. Daddy told him he would go with him if he didn't hurt me. The bad man tied his hands." Jenny was trembling now. "Daddy told me to stay in the truck until you came."

Cub was very angry. He loaded them both in his truck and drove fast to Cass's and called Beth to come to Cass's house to stay with Mariah and Jenny while he and the sheriff look for Cass. He called the sheriff to meet him at Cass's.

"The sheriff and I will go look for Cass. You must stay home. Beth will come and stay with you. You must stay in the house," Cub said insisting firmly.

"No, I have to go look for him. Grey is going to use him to get the white lion. I have to stop him," Mariah said, tearing up. "You have to let me look for him."

"NO!" shouted Cub.

Mariah's heart sank. She would have to find a way out of the house and back to the truck. She had seen the keys were still in it and getting the truck back to the house wasn't either of the men's priorities.

Beth showed up as promised to watch Mariah and Jenny while the men looked for Cass. Mariah heard Cub say to the sheriff it would be like looking for a needle in a haystack, but they had to try. Mariah knew deep in her heart they wouldn't find him. She had to try to get away. She would sneak out when she could.

"I am going to put Jenny to bed," Mariah told Beth after the sheriff and Cub left. Her plan was to wait until Jenny fell asleep and sneak out the back door without Beth seeing her. She would walk down the road where the truck was left. She was sure the keys were left in it. She repeated this over and over to herself, not sure what she would do if they weren't there.

Jenny quickly fell asleep and sneaking out the back door was easy. Beth sat in the front room and Mariah was sure Beth didn't hear her leave.

Mariah turned the truck and went the opposite way the sheriff and Cub went. She drove a while until she saw the white lion on the road. She stopped and the white lion started walking down another road that forked off to the right. It was an old logging road, and looked like it was not used a lot. Did he want her to follow him? She stopped the truck and the lion stopped. Both stared at each other. He was telling her to go up this old road, right? A strange feeling told her this was the way, so she turned the truck on the road the lion was on. Once she turned on the road, the lion went back into the underbrush. She drove for a long time on the old road, turning when the white lion appeared on forked road, showing her the way. She was miles from the town now. Finally, she could see a dim cabin light high up the mountain. Yes, this might be the place, she thought. She turned her headlights off and slowly climbed out of the truck. The thought of the white lion being out there never crossed her mind again. Mariah was in full-blown search mode. She was, however, very concerned about alerting Grey if this was where he was keeping Cass.

When she got to the cabin, she could see lantern lights through the window. Creeping up to the window she looked in to see Cass tied to a chair, and his face was bloody and cut. Her heart did a flip. She wasn't sure he was alive because his head was down on his chest. Mariah's heart sank, then she felt a gun in her side. She could smell the sickening order of Grey's body odor.

"My lucky day—I got the prize! Never did I ever think I would get you again. How in the heck did you find us?" Grey took her by the arm and tied her up to a tree about fifteen feet from the cabin door. He opened the cabin door so Cass could see her. "Now, Cass you can see her die when the white lion comes for her. I will be waiting for him and shoot him after he kills her," Grey taunted him.

He was alive, Mariah sighed. She started to cry. His face was beat up and swollen. Her heart went into her throat. Things were not looking so good for them. She stopped her crying and said to herself she must not let Grey see her so weak.

Cass looked up to see Mariah tied to the tree. Their eyes met. Cass was OK with Grey killing him, but not Mariah. "Grey, I will give you anything you want. Just untie us and let us go. I will even help you kill the lion for his pelt," Cass begged, knowing he probably killed old Charlie and now knew what he was capable of. He was mad at himself for not thinking about this place. It was miles up the larger mountain and very remote. Charlie's cabin was the only one on this road.

Grey laughed his almost toothless grin. "You are in no position to ask for anything. This little darling is the lion's magnet. He will be here, and I don't need you or anyone else." Grey slapped his leg. "Oh, this could not get any better."

Cass looked up again at Mariah. Grey was right. She was the lion's magnet. He wished he had told her how he felt about her. His heart now ached; he should have told her he had fallen in love with her. He was surprised as to how calm Mariah appeared now. Her crying had stopped and now she raised her chin in defiance. Mariah was about to meet her death and looked at him with a strength that calmed him.

"Cass, it is going to be OK. I know very little about love or men. I want to let you know I think I have fallen in love with you and I want to make sure I tell you this before—before we die—even if you are not in love with me," Mariah said bravely. She shot Grey a look of disgust and continued. "I knew I loved you, but I have been too afraid to say anything for fear of your rejection. Now I wish I had."

"I also have fell in love with you," he said, as he smiled at her with his swollen face and continued. "I am sorry. If we ever get out of this alive, will you marry me?"

Mariah's heart warmed as she said, "I would love to marry you. I would love to be Jenny's mom." Her voice cracked when she said Jenny. She thought of the young child she had become so attached to. If anything happened to them, she would be alone. No, she thought, that's not right. Cass's family would make sure she would be taken care of. This thought strengthened her more.

The thought had already crossed Cass's mind earlier before Mariah had showed up. He had felt Mariah would have stayed and cared for Jenny if anything had happened to him but now, he thought of Jenny mourning them both and his head fell forward as a tear ran down his face.

"We will survive, Cass. I have dreamed this," Mariah told him the small lie. "Don't give up. Stay strong for Jenny, for me," she encouraged.

Grey laughed at this and said, "How are you going to survive? The lion will smell you and come for you. After he kills you and I kill him I plan on killing Cass. But I want him to see you die first. You have not a chance in hell of getting out of this one. Just when I thought it could not get any better!"

The lion roamed through the underbrush around the cabin. He could smell them. Something made him watch as Grey tied Mariah up. Something summoned him to go down the mountain again.

Cub and the sheriff had turned their vehicle around after Beth figured out Mariah was gone. She told them Mariah had gone the opposite way they had went. Beth didn't hear Mariah leave the house. The old truck could be heard loudly as it barreled down road and this is when Beth knew Mariah had snuck out of the house.

The sheriff was a little concerned with her going this way due to the poor road conditions and the small and numerous forks and turns. It would be hard to figure out which road to take.

"What was she thinking?" the sheriff asked Cub. "She has no weapon and that damn lion probably hasn't eaten for a couple of days. It could be looking for a meal."

They drove up the mountain looking for lights or any kind of a clue. Suddenly when they went around a corner the road forked. On the right side of the fork the white lion appeared, and it sat there looking back at them.

"Jesus, let me get my rifle!" the sheriff cried.

"No! I think he is trying to tell us something," Cub said. "Few men have ever seen the lion. He wants us to turn on this road."

"You're kidding. Aren't you? This is a man-killer and we have the chance to kill it!" the sheriff yelled.

Calmly Cub put his hand on the sheriff's arm and said, "Look closely. The lion is not moving. He sits there waiting for us. Turn the truck toward the road the lion is on."

As he did the lion slowly walked the road in front of them for a while and went back into the woods. Both men looked at each other and continued down the road the lion had led them on. Again, they came to a forked road. These were old logging roads with deep holes and washouts. The sheriff stopped the vehicle and again the lion appeared on the road to his right. When the sheriff turned down the road the lion again went into the forest.

Shaking his head, the sheriff said, "I don't believe it. Do you think he is leading us to where Mariah is? I just don't believe it."

CHAPTER THIRTY

Grey sat on the porch close to the door of the cabin where he could watch the lion attack Mariah. He laughed at the fact the dumb asses were not going to ever be together. He laughed out loud, knowing it must be true love and he was going to destroy it. This was going to be so rewarding, he thought, smiling to himself. Something about that made him happy. But he wanted to touch Mariah, maybe in front of Cass? This would be the ultimate reward for him! Laughing, he got up and walked over to the tree. Mariah looked at him defiantly. Grey said to her in a low voice, "If the lion doesn't come, I will shoot both of you and bury you by old Charlie in the back of the cabin. No one would ever know. We are so far up the mountain in the thick woods no one would ever think to look here. How did you find me?" He untied her and pushed her toward the cabin. Before he got to the cabin, he tripped her, and towered over her on the ground.

"Tell me how you found me?" he asked again.

"The white lion led me here," she said, waiting for him to laugh.

"I should take you here in front of your lover," Grey said, loud enough for Cass to hear. "If your lion is close, he will watch."

Cass worked the ropes that tied his hands together. They were tied so tight it was cutting off his circulation. "Grey! Don't touch her! You must listen to me. I can make you a rich man," begged Cass. Grey laid his rifle down by Mariah. Mariah rolled away from him and hoped it was far enough where Cass couldn't see what was about to happen to her. Grey finally caught her and fell on her. When he started trying to undo her jeans she screamed and pleaded, "Please, don't. Don't!" She continued to scream, hoping the white lion would hear them.

The white lion's scream stopped Grey. He stood up quickly and looked around. Mariah no longer had her hands tied and tried to stand up.

"Wow here comes your kitty," Grey announced. "Get down on the ground," he instructed. He pulled her to her knees, and she fell forward. "Now stay here."

Grey went to sit back on the porch in his chair. He instructed Mariah to stay there on the ground or he would cause her to bleed and reminded her he could shoot her in the leg, which would get the lion there faster. "Also remember your lover has already bled all over. This is probably what the lion smells," Grey said and laughed to himself.

The sheriff and Cub followed the old logging road up the mountain, turning on roads the white lion was on. The trees grew high over the road and there were many washouts, making the truck bounce.

"Up there!" Cub shouted. "It's Cass's truck."

"Yes, I see it. Why would she stop here?" questioned the sheriff. He still could not believe the white lion had directed them up here. Were they headed into a trap?

Both got out of the truck and stood by Cass's truck, looking up the mountain. Then they both saw a small light through the trees.

"That is old Charlie Harris's cabin. Hmm, a good place to get out of sight. Never crossed my mind Grey would venture this far up the mountain. We will walk up the rest of the way," said the sheriff. "Do you have a gun? You know that white lion could be out there watching us," said the sheriff.

"No, I don't have a gun and the white lion led us here. He is not going to bother us. He is probably looking right now at Mariah, waiting for us to get there," Cub insisted. "I know you don't believe it, but he has led us to Mariah."

They went through underbrush and it was slow going. Both jumped when they heard Mariah scream, and then a scream from the white lion. Both stopped and looked at each other and without a word started to run through the undergrowth.

Back at the cabin Mariah sat up from the ground, looking directly at Grey. She wasn't going to give up. She didn't think the lion would hurt her, but he would Cass. She went to stand. Grey stood up and walked over to her, threating her to stay still. He grabbed her arm and pushed her, making her fall on the ground. She didn't care if he shot her. She had her hands free and she planned on charging him. Mariah stopped trying to get up when she saw movement to her right. The white lion was creeping toward them. As she watched him, their eyes locked. She sat down on the ground again. The white lion was the first to look away and he crept slowly toward them. Grey stood over her with the gun aimed at her heart, enjoying knowing he was in full control. He had no idea the lion was stalking him. In the flash of an eye the large cat jumped Grey from behind. His rifle flew out of his hands next to Mariah. She could hear bones crunch when the lion sank his teeth into Grey's neck. Grey let out a scream but soon had gone limp. The lion stepped off the body. He sniffed the air and turned and started to go toward the cabin door. Mariah grabbed the rifle and shot twice in the air. The lion turned and looked at her and turned back to the cabin. She had never shot a gun or even held one, so this really surprised her, but her goal was to save Cass. She raised the gun and shot two times into the white lion. It fell to the ground. Red blood started to flow onto the white fur. Mariah took a deep ragged breath.

"I'm sorry; I can't let you hurt him," she said as she dropped the gun. She ran into the cabin and untied Cass.

He stood up and hugged her and softly said, "I saw the lion attack Grey and thought he would attack you, but he didn't. He was coming for me. You saved my life. Thank you." He continued to hug her. "I love you," he said and kissed her lightly with his bruised lips. It felt good to finally admit it and say it to her.

Cub and the sheriff heard the four shots and arrived at the cabin a short time later. When they got there, they saw Grey and the white lion laying on the ground but no Mariah or Cass.

"Cass! Mariah!" the sheriff yelled.

"Yes, we are in here," Cass said, laughing. He still had Mariah in his arms, and he wasn't going to let her go.

Both Cub and the sheriff were relieved to see both alive. Both sighed a breath of relief when they entered the cabin.

"Cub, Cub, it's the most unbelievable thing. The white lion led me up here. I just had a feeling I was going the right way and when I wasn't sure he came out from the underbrush and showed me which way to go." Tears filled her eyes as she said, "I had to kill him. He was going for Cass after he jumped Grey." Mariah was surprised to feel very sad that she had end the life of the beautiful beast. It saved her and Cass's lives.

"Well, you're never going to believe it, but he did the same for the sheriff and me," Cub reported to her.

"He was going for Cass, so I shot him," Mariah said sadly again. "I was forced to do it." She now was crying.

"You saved my life. You are very brave," Cass said. "You and only you were the one to kill the lion. Mariah, he was a man-killer. Remember?"

The massive cat lay in front of the cabin. It took three of them to move the lion. Cub had gone back to the truck and drove it up the mountain. All three men lifted the cat to put him in the truck. They used an old rug to wrap Grey's body up to take it back to town. They found Nooka's white lion pelt in good shape and Cub said he would take it back to her.

"Doc and I will have to come back later and make sure old Charlie is buried so the animals don't get him. He would have wanted to be buried on his property. All of Grey's dogs have been shot and are in the shed out back. He must have not wanted them to make any noise. We will have to bury them too," offered the sheriff.

Cass and Mariah rode home with the sheriff. Mariah held a cloth on Cass's cut above his eye to stop the bleeding. He looked at her with his good eye and said, "I meant what I asked you. Do you really want to marry me?"

Mariah smiled and said, "Yes. I fell in love with you the night of the water leak. When you touched me, I just knew but I didn't want to admit it. I am inexperienced with love and really didn't understand until tonight that it was love. Previously before tonight you just seemed like you didn't want to be around me. So, I hid my feelings."

Cass sighed and said, "I couldn't trust myself around you. I was so drawn to you. But when I lost my wife, it hurt too badly. It was one of the hardest things I ever had to do trying to stay away from you. I myself didn't think I loved you until I saw Grey hurt you and plan to kill us both. It made me admit to myself I loved you from the minute I first saw you asleep on my porch. Too bad it took this to admit and say I love you." He lightly kissed Mariah on the forehead with his bruised and cut lips. She smiled up at him.

The sheriff was smiling. He was so relieved he and Cub had found them before something happened. He remembered the white lion and how it helped with the search. It was unbelievable how the lion had helped find Cass and Mariah.

It was almost dawn when the sheriff, Cass, and Mariah drove up to the front of Doc's house. They had to wake Doc. He sleepily staggered out of the house but really woke up when he saw Cass's face.

"What on earth happened?" Doc asked when the shock wore off. "Come in here so I can sew you up."

The sheriff explained the whole night to Doc while he was stitching Cass up. Doc smiled the whole time, very aware of how Cass and Mariah now looked at each other. He wanted to say something but thought better of it. This was great, and he didn't want this to change! Doc looked Mariah over and found only scraps and a lot of bruising.

The sheriff took the white lion's body over to Nooka's. There Cub would skin and bury the rest of the animal in Nooka's backyard. Later, the tribe would celebrate that the valley was rid of the white lion.

When Cass and Mariah were dropped off at Cass's house Jenny came running out and stopped short when she saw her daddy's face. Cass picked up the shocked child and sat down with her on the porch.

"Daddy, you beat the bad man up, didn't you?" asked a very serious Jenny. "I told you, Beth." Jenny turned to tell Beth.

Beth had stepped outside on the porch with them but didn't say anything. She sat down to listen to the story of their evening of terror.

Sadly, Beth acknowledged the white lion was dead. She was a little sad but now she could go back to Africa and spend time with the man she loved. She had enjoyed coming back to the area she was born in, but now was the time to go back to Africa and tell Brian she loved him, that she would marry him and his have children. She was ready. They might just have to move to the valley, she thought.

Mariah and Cass slept until late afternoon. Beth had stayed to watch Jenny. Spending time with Jenny made Beth really want children. The child was a delight and so smart.

Late afternoon Cass got up first, and later Mariah. Both wore bruises and cuts from the night before.

"I just made some coffee, sleepy heads," Beth told them. "I am going to have to go break up my camp and pay my team. Also, help yourselves to the dinner I made in the oven."

"That would be great!" said Cass. "Wait a minute, Beth. Sit down please. Jenny, Mariah and I have something to tell you."

Jenny went over to her father and said, "What is it, Daddy?"

"Well, Mariah and I want you to know we are getting married!" Cass exclaimed to her.

Jenny jumped into his arms and asked, "She will be my new mommy?"

"Yes, will that be OK?" Cass asked. "We don't have a date yet, but can you be our flower girl?"

Jenny started crying. Cass looked at Mariah for help.

Mariah asked Jenny, "You don't want me to be your new mommy?"

Jenny nodded her head yes and shouted, "Oh yes. I would just love it! This is a happy cry."

They all started laughing.

Beth left after congratulating them, "I am so happy for you both. I would like to be notified of the date so I can come back with Brian, my boyfriend. I plan on marrying him and I just might ask if I can do it in your backyard! It is beautiful." Beth shook Cass's hand and hugged Mariah. "I will be calling my uncle later for updates!"

Later there was a knock on the door and Mariah opened it to let Cub and Nooka in. Cub helped Nooka sit down in a chair. She looked very tired but had begged Cub to take her to see Mariah. "You have done well," Nooka said as she patted Mariah's hand. "You were able to kill the white lion. Your dream came true and you made the perfect ending to it."

It occurred to Mariah she had not had time to tell Cass she was Nooka's great grandchild. She turned to Cass and explained.

"So, is Nooka my grandma?" asked Jenny. Everyone laughed.

"When I marry your daddy, my great-grandma Nooka will be your great-great-grandma and Cub will be your cousin," explained Mariah. This delighted Jenny and she went and hugged them both.

When Cass's family found out about their upcoming wedding plans the entire family came over all at once. The house was full. Mariah looked at her new family and never thought she would ever be this happy. It was hard to accept when her mother died that she had no family left. She smiled to herself thinking of when she stood by her mother's grave and felt so alone. The valley had given her the gift of family and she would never feel that way again.

Cass's sisters-in-law helped Mariah plan the wedding and pick out her dress.

Cass decided Beth's idea of having a wedding in the backyard was an excellent idea. It would be midsummer, and the backyard would hold many people, he thought.

They were married by the lake. The lake was still, and it mirrored the mountains behind it.

Several tents, tables, and chairs were set up for their guests. Cass's brothers were his groomsman, and Cub was his best man. Cass's sisters-in-law were Mariah's bridesmaids and Jamie her maid of honor. It was a beautiful wedding. Jenny was the flower girl and Wolf the ring bearer.

A band played after the wedding and everyone danced.

Doc danced with Jenny most of the night until he tired and then Cub took over. Jamie put Jenny to bed and waited for her to go to sleep before returning to dance with Cub.

Liz had closed McCain's and came to the wedding. Her knee-length dress was a bright blue and covered her breasts. She had minimal makeup on and really looked like a pretty young woman.

As the band played Liz sang several songs she and Mariah had chosen. Over the past several weeks Liz and Mariah had developed a close friendship. When pictures were taken Mariah had asked for a picture of just her and Liz.

The next day after the wedding Mariah sat on the back porch by Cass, with Jenny sleeping in his arms. They sat on the screened in porch looking over the lake. She remembered the dreams that had gotten her to this beautiful place. The yellow eyes she could not figure out, haunting her dreams. Now she knew what pulled her here. A feeling of serenity hit her, and she was happy. She told Cass she wanted to start a family right away and he agreed immediately.

"Jenny needs a little brother or sister," Mariah told Cass as she smiled up at him and asked, "Maybe two or three?"

Cass laughed and hugged her saying, "That would be OK." He was thankful for her. He looked at his small daughter sleeping in his arms. "I never thought I would be happy again. All thanks to the white lion."

Up high in the mountain the female lion was about to give birth. She had prepared the small cave only days before. She labored for most of the night and at dawn she bore the first-born, which was a female. The second born was a very large male and he was white.

CPSIA information can be obtained
at www.ICGtesting.com
Printed in the USA
LVHW040201140120
643548LV00006B/554/P